BEX KESIA

Diddly Tales

Bex Kesia

Contents

Introduction

Diddly Tales, Anais Nin, and Masturbation.
Welcome to Diddly Tales. My name is Bex, and this is a memoir of erotic shorts chronicling a journey of sexual discovery and exploration spanning continents and decades. Raised in Ghana, America, Nigeria, Turkey, Pakistan, China, Swaziland, and Italy, my international upbringing exposed me to an array of cultures, and people, which in turn opened the door to exciting sexual experiences. As a young woman awakening to the new sights, sounds, and smells of puberty, I was hungry to feel and understand every bit of pleasure, even though I was ignorant of how it could be derived. My initial introduction to sexuality was found in the deep recesses of my father's library in Ankara, Turkey, which was home to a menagerie of international authors collected from across the globe. One that drew me into its hold was *Delta of Venus: Erotica by Anais Nin (1977)*. This collection of erotic stories awakened my sexuality, opening the doors to my need to know more, feel more, and see more. My imagination was limitless as my attractions were to both men and women, and I was in awe of all the unique ways in which beauty existed in so many forms. Through the mind of Anais, I learned that sexual desires are uniquely different for everyone, and it was within

1

those pages, that I experienced the sweet desire to touch myself. The lesson was that between my legs lay a little nub of skin that when touched properly, would open deep wells of pleasure and a world of infinite elation. This simple act of masturbation would open an avenue to connection with myself and others . To be connected to one's pleasure center and honor it as the gem it is, is to understand that diddling is a form of worship, and diddly tales a form of scripture. Blessed be the fruit, and we all know that in sex, the female form bears the most beautiful fruit, the clitoris.

I share with you a collection of stories called Diddly tales.

What is a Diddly Tale?

In the Urban Dictionary, to *Diddle is to touch or caress the genitals in some way; stimulation to the clit, mostly in female masturbation, but can also apply when someone else is joined in the stimulation.*

Therefore a 'Diddly Tale' is a story that awakens sexual desire and leads to masturbation. To Diddle oneself is to touch one's erogenous zones to orgasm. The following Diddly tales are meant to help you do just that.

I share these stories with you as an opportunity to enjoy, learn and experience the beautiful ways in which love, sex, connection, fantasy, and experimentation add to a fulfilling life. These stories are for those who enjoy exploring sexuality in all its glorious blunders, and for those who want to see the world through a woman's lens. It is for the ones who have embraced the knowledge that women's pleasure, and safety in exploring that pleasure, are as deserved as being loved. So, I want to be

2

clear, this is NOT a story about finding the one.

This story is about being the one.

The one who wants to experience all the pleasures life has to offer a bisexual, biracial, spiritually free woman.

Buckle up and feel free to diddle yourself at any time!

"Her elongated eyes did not close as other women's eyes did, but like the eyes of tigers, pumas and leopards, the two lids meeting lazily and slowly . . ."
— Anais Nin, *Delta of Venus*

The information presented is the author's opinion and does not constitute any health or medical advice. The content of this book is for entertainment purposes only and is not intended to diagnose, treat, cure, or prevent any condition or disease, nor does it guarantee an orgasm.

The First Kiss

I n the binary world, my first kiss came at the sweet age of fourteen at the Ikoyi club in Lagos, Nigeria. He was half Vietnamese and half white, and we had met in school attracted to the mixed nature of our origins. My Ghanaian mother's royal black skin and my American father's Jewish white pale had produced golden children seen as exotic and beautiful in a world divided by race.

We had spent the day swimming at the private club, innocently flirting, and stuffing our faces with the best spicy grilled Suya meat in Lagos. Under the hot African sun, his tan skin glowed, and we were both in awe of the way the water made us sparkle. Catching him staring, our eyes would lock, big grins spreading across our faces. He was beautiful, with wavy black hair that glistened, and an aura of golden spiced honey.

As the day waned, we were due to be picked up by our respective drivers. Waiting out front of the rotary club, as the long lines of Peugeot and land cruisers pulled up to pick up their guests, I spotted my driver. Quickly turning my head to bid my date farewell, I felt lips press against the side of my face as he accidentally kissed my eye. I was startled as my brain attempted to understand what was happening and why he was so close. As I looked him in the face he came in for another kiss, landing puckishly on my lips. I closed my eyes, as I had seen ladies do in the movies, and that's when I felt it. A little explosion went off in my body as a new shot of hormones ignited from his touch. And then it was over. I opened my eyes and as I gazed into his, a bloom of emotion crossed my face; and I felt a haziness in the air. Finally, my first kiss! It was hard-core teen-crushing, a new and exhilarating feeling to experience. Or was it new? Was this truly my first kiss?

A year prior, I had become friends with a new girl whose family had arrived from the American South with a twang in her voice and lips that moved like molasses. I was entranced by her mannerisms and began to adopt her speech and quirky colloquialisms. "Ain't" being a favorite word, I laughed at the ease with which she added "Ain't I, ain't he, ain't she, ain't they?" at the end of every comment. 'She's pretty, ain't she?' 'He's dumb as bricks, ain't he?' Always turning to me for a second opinion, confirmation, or validation of our shared perspective. And I would giggle agreeably. We spent lazy afternoons after school lounging on her play bed, daydreaming and discussing the strange nature of boys. Like most teens, that grew up in the 1980's we had been fed stylistically dramatic teen love stories filled with dreamy boys sporting feathered hairstyles, and awkward geeks who could not catch a break. *Sixteen Candles, The Breakfast Club, Pretty in Pink* (looking at you John Hugh's!!) We shared fantasies of romantic possibilities with boys from our class, all the while hugging and delicately exploring each other's skin. We would delight in little kisses with the belief that practice would ensure we were ready when the time came for our "FIRST KISS"

Looking back at the ease with which we touched, caressed, and explored the soft lines and supple nature of our developing bodies, I now realize this was an awakening. Opening to the new sensations of sexual touch, and the haze of innocent desire led us to soft kisses and limbs gingerly intertwined in puppy love, and what I now deem "My First Kiss."

Headfirst into Lessons

If I told you I lost my virginity to the class clown, would you laugh? I was in my sophomore year of high school in Ankara, Turkey. We lived in Cankaya, a cosmopolitan neighborhood perched high up on the side of the bowl that cradles the city below. Living amongst the Turks was a gift, as their culture, food, and hospitality opened the door to truly unique experiences. Eating at a Turkish restaurant meant you could pick from a wide range of little *meze* platters to share. A waiter would bring out a giant platter of little dishes; creamy whipped lemon hummus with black salt-cured olives delicately nestled with drizzles of pure virgin olive oil. Smokey fire pit roasted eggplant, blended scrumptiously into a dip and served with kiln-baked pita bread. Followed by an entree of *Iskender*, charred lamb slices laid on a bed of grilled pita and topped with sizzling hot butter and a tangy tomato sauce. The flavors are so divine, my soul momentarily leaves my body at first bite. This was the spice of life in Ankara and the new sights, sounds, and sensations spurred me into sensual explorations.

I met Liam in school, and as the class clown I must admit, he was a laugh. He managed to break up the monotony of school days with a well-placed comment, mid-lesson. It would pull me out of my daydreams and into a fit of laughs along with the rest of the class. The fly in every teacher's ointment, he seemed on the road to failure, but somehow his charm always got him out of trouble. Towering over the other boys his age by a good five inches, and with a full head of feathery brown hair flecked with blond highlights, his style mirrored the teen bop pin-up boys of the 1980's. I was heavily mainlining *Christian Slater* movies at the time, so of course he caught my eye.

As one of the token "nerds" in the class, I had absolutely no expectations of ever being seen by him, so imagine my surprise when he started hanging around and intentionally cracking jokes, to make me smile. How did I know it was for my amusement? Because he said he liked watching me laugh. After a brief flirtation, he asked me to be his girlfriend, and as a young, mixed teen in a predominantly white world, I was flattered to be seen by someone who I deemed hotter and cooler than myself. Our interactions had been limited as any rendezvous meant we had to steal away behind closed doors during babysitting sessions, which I found out the hard way, to be a risky endeavor. It was one such afternoon when Liam was asked to watch his younger brother after school. I too had been tasked by my parents to do the same with my brother, and realizing our good fortune we opted to babysit them together. We headed over to Liam's house, and after parking our siblings in front of the TV for an afternoon of gaming, he and I stole away to the back bedroom, to fool around.

Shutting the door behind us, we were in our world as he caressed my cheek, ran his finger down the side of my neck, and pulled me into a soft kiss. He stole my breath as I began to sink into his ever-enveloping arms. Opening my lips, his tongue caressed mine as he nibbled and sucked, leaving them plump. I bit his lower lip playfully, which led him to emit a groan of pleasure. The sound teetered off into a growl that made a fire rise within my pussy. Rubbing my hands down his front, I reached for his crotch, finding a fully erect bulge bursting through his jeans, demanding attention. Rubbing it vigorously, I watched as his eyes went wild and he grabbed onto my shoulders, his legs going weak. I took this opportunity to unzip him, and with one swift movement, I dropped his pants and boxers to his ankles. Gingerly pushing him back onto the bed, his erect penis glistened, reaching out as if to say "Please, please, please touch me." I dropped to my knees, staring in surprise. Gripping his hips, I was so turned on, I wanted to put it in my mouth, and so I did.

The soft skin on his bulbous head surprised me, as I languished licking it, flicking my tongue, before popping the whole head into my mouth and sucking it like a lollipop. This was my first time giving head, and I must say, I thoroughly enjoyed it. With each lick and suck, I felt my panties get wetter, as the sounds of his groans rippled through my body causing it to ignite at the pleasure of feeling him in the throes of his passion. I felt a control as if I was the maestro of his elation, and the symphony was just building. Arching his back, he leaned away, gasping each time I plunged his fat penis deep into the back of my throat. I was insatiable, attempting to fit the entire cock in my mouth, while making little swallow movements, threatening to gulp it whole. I could taste little bits of salty precum drizzle from the tip and was delighted by it. I reached for his balls which had pulled themselves taught just under his shaft and delicately fondled them, curious as to how hard I might squeeze. We were deep in the throes of pleasure when the door swung open, and a spotlight illuminated the scene within. This light seemed to split open the dark room, as Liam pushed me away, hurriedly attempting to conceal his nakedness. The movement caught me wholly off guard as I had closed my eyes, lost in the carnal pleasures of passion. Being thrown back onto the floor, I was momentarily blinded, unaware that his mother had just walked in on us to find my head perfectly buried in her son's crotch.

"Get dressed and get out here" was all she said, before flipping on the overhead light and shutting the door. We both stood, staring at the door and then at each other as the shock began to settle. My face, which had been hot with passion, grew even hotter with embarrassment. I wiped my mouth, as he hurriedly pulled up his pants, scrambling to appear decent. I reached for the door, but before I could turn the knob, he grabbed my arm and pulled me back into his embrace, once again. Kissing me on the forehead, the cheek, and then my lips, he very softly whispered "Thank you, and I'm so sorry. I should have locked the door". We proceeded to giggle in hushed tones as our bodies shook, and our hearts beat in both elation and panic. This little gesture made me feel a little less shame at having been caught, and with the knowledge of our shared guilt, we walked out of that room, hand in hand, ready to face the whip.

As we entered the living room, his mother looked up and said it was time for my brother and I to head home. As to whether our siblings were aware of our little indiscretion, I was too uncomfortable to care, and hurriedly shooed my brother to the exit. Liam's mother turned to him and said, "Don't you think you should walk her out, and make sure she gets into a cab?". The expression on her face was amusingly critical, as if he should know better. This little question was a lesson that would forever stay with me. He stepped forward and opened the front door, for us to pass through. Turning to his mother,

I waved goodbye and caught her trying not to laugh. Taking my hand, he walked us to the curb and hailed one of the bright yellow cars, zipping up and down the street. I looked away, still in disbelief at what had occurred. He opened the car door and let my brother enter before pulling me once more into his arms and kissing me passionately. Whispering in my ear, he said, "I will probably be grounded for a month, so please wait for me". We both laughed, shaking our heads at the absurdity of it all and smiling with the hidden knowledge that there was so much more pleasure to come!

Did you think this was my virginity story? Hah! The joke's on you.

Cosmic Cunnilingus

The first time a man went down on me, I was in Afghanistan. On summer break from university, my older brother and I had been summoned by the family to join them in Islamabad. Although living in Pakistan, my father, a UNICEF representative, spent the work week in Kabul, a journey that required a life-harrowing plane ride to Peshawar in northern Pakistan, and a drive across the Khyber Pass into neighboring Afghanistan. Ensconced in war and under the yoke of Taliban rule, Afghanistan was a dangerous place to play, but having been exposed to the carjacking streets of Lagos, we were accustomed to strife-filled countries. I was curious to see the real conditions under extremist Islamic rule and as always, my thirst for exploration led me to join my father on his next jaunt into Taliban country.

After landing in Peshawar in northern Pakistan, we were pawned off on my father's work colleague, a Lebanese gentleman named Levi. He had a dark, full head of hair that looked like it had been styled by a Land Rover on some dusty back road; an effect that made his rugged looks seem effortless. Standing at 6'3", he was a good head and shoulders taller than the surrounding populace, which had been stunted by malnutrition and the scarcities that war zones inflict. His rumpled jeans and well-worn shirt with the sleeves rolled up belied a need for comfort over diplomacy.

We had set out early in the morning to make the journey from Peshawar in northern Pakistan across the Khyber Pass into neighboring Afghanistan. My father had taken a different path, heading to the capital, intent to stay in Kabul for the night and meet us the following day. Due to the dangerous nature of the region, my brother, Levi, and myself were headed across the border towards Darin, a province, known for its tribal lands and border villages. Fortuitously for me, this area was out of the direct eye of the Taliban mullahs, or religious police, who banned women from being in public spaces. The day had begun uneventfully, in part due to the heavily armed guards that milled around the Hotel in Peshawar, a sight I had grown accustomed to. As I walked out the front entrance to meet our driver, I passed a sign instructing that all guests must check their firearms. It was a coat check for your weapons. I can only imagine the ruckus that had led to such a necessity. Piling into the Jeep with 'United Nations' emblazoned on the sides, we made our way out of town.

The roads were barren as we made the two-hour drive, and I happily bounced in my seat when we hit an occasional pothole, immersed in a feeling of *vorfreude*. Levi and my brother were discussing the history of the region and I would pipe in to add my two cents on the Russian invasion and subsequent retreat.

Having studied it in school the semester prior, I peppered Levi with questions about women's rights and their access to education, subsequently forcing him to turn around and look at me. At one point he stopped speaking mid-sentence and said "You have a curious mind". I blushed and replied, "You know a lot". I felt a twinge of desire between my legs, as we kept our

13

eyes locked, and I did not want to look away. The moment was broken when our driver informed us, we were approaching the border checkpoint.

This is where the real adventure kicked off, as our UN vehicle was stopped, searched and our passports handed over to security. The guard entered a small wooden shed as his cohorts milled around the car, peaking in to catch glimpses of the beautiful, young, dark woman who sat in the back seat. I was wearing blue jeans, a white button-down, and a baseball cap with my hair pulled back into a loose bun. As I turned to look out the window, I saw one guard's jaw drop to the ground like a Tom and Jerry cartoon. I averted my gaze, uncomfortably. Emerging from the shed, the main guard returned and held up our passports. As Levi reached through the window, the guard held the documents aloft and began barking commands. He looked at me and repeated his command. I could sense the tension in the air, and froze, not understanding what was happening and yet trying to maintain my composure. Levi raised his voice repeatedly saying "UN Diplomat! UN Diplomat!" as the soldiers surrounding the vehicle clutched their automatic weapons tightly. Seeing that Levi would not back down, the guard handed over our passports and waved us through with a look of anger.

We were a good way down the road, with the checkpoint clearly out of view, before anyone spoke. My brother asked if they wanted money, as we had seen so many times before. Bribing or "dashing" was a common tithe, that we had experienced at checkpoints in Nigeria, Ghana, Mexico, Egypt, and Turkey, so why not Afghanistan? Levi turned his body 180 degrees, looking me squarely in the eyes, and said, "They wanted the girl". My heart stopped, as I realized the very real and new dangers around me. We were in an Islamic fundamentalist country now, and I was just a piece of property to these men.

As we meandered the dry, brown dusty road towards uncertain adventure, Levi peered back periodically, searching my face. Gone was the inquisitive young woman who had lit up at his glance. The experience made me retreat into the safety of my daydreams.

A good hour and a half passed in silence and introspection, when the road suddenly veered off and a row of three-sided structures of mud brick appeared before us. The Land Rover slowed, idling by the open structures that reminded me of dollhouses, if not for the contents of the rooms. Littered across the floors was a cornucopia of weapons. American M16s, Soviet Ak47s, or Kalashnikovs, as they referred to them. Brain guns, pistols, automatics, semi-automatics, all scattered around, and amid all these weapons sat an elderly man with heavily tanned, leathery wrinkled skin. In his hands, he held small bullet casings which he delicately filled with gunpowder before capping and hammering shut. My brain exploded as it tried to sort out what was happening. 'Was this man hand-making guns and bullets? Was I at an "Artisanal" weapons market? 'Handmade in Afghanistan?'

As we exited the vehicle and made our way gingerly towards the dollhouses, a few men approached and beckoned us towards their wares. This was not my first experience seeing weapons of mass destruction, but it was certainly a surprise to see them so casually handled. They began pulling Kalashnikovs off the floor and handing them over, insisting we try them out. When he overheard my brother and I speak English, he pulled out an M16 and proclaimed it was the "best American gun". This village had been hand-making weapons and selling them locally, ensuring an endless supply to feed all sides of a never-ending civil war.

After overcoming my initial shock at the number of guns, I adopted my game face and took to perusing the stock as if I was shopping at Bergdorf Goodman, impressively feigning over weapons, knowing full well I had no intention of purchasing. A stout, bearded Pashtun gentleman in a blue *pakol* hat held up an AK47 exclaiming, "You shoot! You shoot!". As any good diplomats' kid will tell you, when confronted with local culture, it is best to take part, as to avoid offense, of any nature. Who was I to deny their hospitality?

Beckoning us to follow him out, we made our way up a gravelly path, buttressed with dry needled shrubbery, that had been formed through overuse. Stopping just under a large spindly tree, our host pointed up at the mountain and once again commanded "Shoot! Shoot!". I looked at Levi for reassurance, and he replied deferentially with 'Shoot the mountain". Stepping up, I took the automatic weapon and pointed it at my target. Levi stepped behind me, placing his body behind mine, wrapping his arms around me, and guiding his shoulder to support mine. His scent was a mix of sweat and lemon oil, which surprised me, and as I looked up, I felt his warm breath brush against my forehead. He smiled and said "For the kickback. Just until you get used to it." I turned, aimed for the mountain, took a breath, slowly let it out, and squeezed the trigger. The AK47 shot a multiple stream of bullets sending a wave of power through my right shoulder. The force propelled me back into his chest, which bore the brunt and protected me from slamming against the tree. Now I understood why they picked this spot. How many other adventurers had been thrown down on the jagged pathway below?

Our Pashtun host pointed up at the top of the mountain excitedly, as a goat perched high up on the cliff came into view. Levi spoke softly, directly into my ear, "He wants you to shoot the goat."

They will throw a feast tonight in your honor." The thought of killing something made me tremble with unease, and made Levi look down at me curiously. I replied with a firm "no", pointed the gun at the mountain, and shot at it again.

The rush of force as I felt his chest against my back, sent ripples of pleasure through my body. I liked it, and I wanted more. Sending another wave of bullets flying, I began laughing at the rush of heat building between us. He gripped me tighter, ensuring there was no space between us, and said, "Again". The demand from his lips sent me reeling as I fired off another session of rounds. He held firm with each burst, and when I stopped firing, I felt his body soften and I could feel the weight of him. I handed the gun back to our host and turned to check on Levi. Taking both his hands to help sturdy each other, I asked if he was okay. He grinned and nodded screaming "Very okay". The sound of the gun had deafened our ears, so it took a moment to realize that everyone was staring as Levi and I locked eyes, breathing heavily at the exhilaration of shared energy. He suddenly released one hand and made a gesture of helping me down the pathway. I looked at my brother, whose inquisitive, wide-eyed stare, and cocked head, made me laugh. "You try it. It's dizzying!" I quipped a little too loudly.

The rest of the afternoon was spent shooting various weapons, and gleefully basking in the dangerous energy of it, until we were well drained from the high. When it was time to head out and make our way back to Peshawar, another 3-hour drive, not a word was spoken, as we raced the sun to arrive safely.

After arriving back at the Pearl International Hotel in Peshawar, we agreed to take a short nap before meeting up for dinner. My brother and I shared a room, and he passed out, upon hitting the bed.

I, on the other hand, was too wired from the excitement of the day and opted to go for a swim. The pool was dark and abandoned, which was exactly how I liked it. I wore a black one-piece and picked a chair that was slightly hidden from the entrance by a line of reeds that circled the perimeter. Eager to feel a sense of peace, while floating in a body of water, I knew this would be the remedy to calm my nerves and center my mood. I swam softly, lap after lap, coming up for breath every so often. The quiet water world below pulled me into its hazy dream-like state. As I came up for air by the poolside, I realized that someone was laying on the deck chair next to my towel. As my eyes focused, my body let out a sigh as I realized it was Levi.

"You shouldn't be out here alone. It's not safe", he whispered.

I looked around cautiously, pulling myself out of the pool. "How did you know I was here?" I asked curiously.

"Security called me. Only men can use the pool" he said apologetically.

My brazen spirit fired inside, angry at the thought that I was not to have the same freedoms as the men. He sensed my shift and held the towel open for me to step into. Wrapping it around my body, he looked down into my eyes.

"You have a fire in you. It is beautiful and wild, and you look like you could burn the hearts of any man who dares stand in your way." The compliment sent a rush of heat to my cheeks, as I could feel the passion between us intensify. I reached up and touched his chest, caressing his shirt and searching for the beat of his heart. Drawing little finger circles across his front, he grabbed my hand and pulled me closer. Our faces were inches apart, neither one of us wanting to break the gaze. His eyes danced down to my lips as I parted them slightly, and then we were ablaze, as his lips pressed firmly against mine. He pulled me deeper behind the reeds, hidden from any prying eyes. Kissing me ravenously, I was consumed with wanting more. When he pulled away, we were once again caught in our world of wanting and desire.

"Put on your clothes. we need to get inside," he growled.

I hurriedly donned my dress, as he took my hand and asked, "Do you want to come to my room?"

Capturing his gaze, I nodded "yes", feeling a hint of rebellion course through me, as he led us away from the "men's only" pool.

The journey from pool to room was a blur, as we attempted to move in the shadows, not knowing whose eyes were watching. As he shut the door behind us, I stepped up once again, reaching for him.

The sensory feeling of touch was my motivating drive and I wanted to rub myself all over his large frame. Kissing me deeply once again, he picked me up and carried me towards the bed. I reached down to unbuckle his pants, but he gripped my hands. I looked up, slightly confused, when he explained, "I want to give you pleasure. Tonight is about you. Now let me taste you."

Pulling my shirt dress up over my head, he stroked the errant hairs away from my face. Tracing that finger down my chest, he stopped to pluck my taught nipple as it strained against the wet swimsuit. He slowly began to peel the suit off, as the rush of cool air made my tits stand at attention, and he maneuvered to warm them with his mouth. teasing my nipple between his teeth, I felt a rush of pleasure course through me that made me gasp. I was now standing naked, slightly self-conscious of being the only one in that position. I was weary of anyone being exposed to my vagina, as I had not yet fallen in love with the view down there. Previous comments about 'Brillo style hair' and 'chafing' had not only left me with an expensive waxing habit, but emotional scars, and the desire to hide.

Taking in my naked body he said, "Such a beautiful spirit. Inside and out" and in that moment, I opted to trust.

Laying back across the bed, I boldly spread my legs, welcoming him. He looked down at me and said, "You are stunning". I was thrilled with all the compliments and felt elated at being admired. Dragging his hands up my outer thighs, he dipped his head to kiss the soft skin between them. He placed little pecks as if he was trying to wake her from a nap, and then suddenly his tongue darted out and licked my clitoris, sending a shock wave through my system. Again, he dipped his tongue, but this time, pressing his lips firmly around my pussy and flicking it quickly. My back arched as I grabbed his hair, feeling waves of pleasure course through me again. My eyes were wide with disbelief, as this was the best feeling I had experienced in my 21 years. His tongue was unmerciful, rapidly strumming over my clit, as I felt my senses awaken to this new level of bliss. I pushed my hips up, trying to reach every bit of pleasure, as a deep ache began to form. I wanted to be filled. Grabbing my ass with one hand, he deftly placed two fingers into my wet pussy, making slow circular motions, going deeper with each rotation. My body felt like it was rolling over waves, one moment lifted in total erotic pleasure and the next ground in disbelief that there was a head in between my thighs. Allowing myself to succumb to the pleasure, I was swept away, riding high, when a firework went off in my brain. The feeling rocked my body, as a deep moan erupted out of my mouth. In that moment I felt like I was one with the universe, an exploding star in the cosmos. I began laughing uncontrollably, as the orgasm pulsed over and over like little shock waves, sending spasms through my limbs. Levi pulled himself up, wrapping me in his arms, as I continued to laugh and shake with little gasping sighs. He kissed my forehead, lingering there as I breathed in his lemony scent. Wrapped in a cocoon of bliss, the waves slowly subsided, and my body went limp with satisfaction. Levi gazed down into my face, meeting my blissful smile with one of his own, and whispered "Beautiful".

The Joy of Toys

I have always been grateful for being introduced to sex toys in my early twenties. I can't imagine how many decades of orgasms I would have missed, had I not. It was the turn of the century (2001), and I was invited to England to join Parker, a gentleman I had met at the high-end restaurant, Asia de Cuba in New York City. We had had a platonic whirl-wind winter romance over the Christmas holiday, which upon his departure back to England, had left us wanting more. To quench this desire, he purchased my plane ticket and insisted I come to visit his manor estate in Guildford, a highly affluent area of Surrey.

The flight was exciting and nerve-racking as we had been apart for over a month, and the anticipation of touching was stirring new desires in me. Picking me up from the airport, he greeted me with a warm hug.

This being the first real physical contact between us, my body lingered in the embrace, until my mind reminded me that I just got off an 8-hour flight and desperately needed a shower. Releasing me from his arms, Parker looked down at me with a smile and said "I am so happy you agreed to come see me. I have had you on my mind all month. I can't get you out of my head." I blushed, laughing at the compliment, and replied "You and I suffer from the same affliction. Thank you for inviting me." Taking my luggage, he grabbed my hand and led the way to his car.

I was riding high as we made our way from the airport to his home, a stone manor house, inadequately titled 'The Sparrow', with massive green lawns that stretched back into moss-covered English woods. The tennis courts were perfectly manicured, and his collection of cars gleamed in the five-car garage. He was tall, standing at 6'2", with black hair and shockingly blue eyes which were set a little too close together giving him an owlish look. His nose had a noticeable bend and stood crookedly on his face, due to a deviated septum, which forced his voice to whine nasally. His body was lean, except for a slightly plump ass, which according to him, was the ruin of all his European cut pants, as it made the pockets puff out, just so.

Our first evening, after so many weeks apart, was a little awkward, as this was a re-introduction. The sheen of holiday lights was no longer glistening, therefore all we had left were our fantasies, and the reality of the present moment. Whisking me away to an old stone brick inn set with a roaring fireplace, we enjoyed a proper English meal of shepherd's pie and were feeling drunk and heavy with red wine.

The conversation had been stimulating and at the same time cozy, as our intimacy grew. By the time dinner ended, my desire was brimming over, and as he drove his Porsche through the winding roads of Surrey, I reached my hand over and laid it affectionately on his leg. He reached down and squeezed it, stroking my thumb, before raising it to his lips and planting a kiss. Gently laying my hand back in his lap, I began rubbing and caressing, slowly moving my hand up his thigh before stopping at the crease; so as not to disturb his driving. He looked down at my hand and then at me. He then proceeded to take my hand and plant it firmly on the bulge of his crotch.

I smiled impishly stroking the firm spot below his jeans. As his package grew, he looked over hungrily and said, "You did that to me". The thought that I had the power to make this man come undone turned me on, spurring me to unzip his pants. He leaned back, pulling his boxer briefs down slightly, as his disgorged member popped up from the folds of fabric. It was hooded, as he was uncircumcised, typical of the English, and I could see his fat pink head peeking out from the rolls of foreskin.

Peeling it down, I proceeded to stroke it, as he gasped in delight and tapped the break. I said "Sorry" to which he replied, "Never apologize for giving me pleasure." Considering that consent, I leaned down and laid my head on his lap. Staring at the plump pink head, I slowly licked the tip, before wrapping my lips around it. He grunted, breathing rapidly, as I felt his penis enlarge in my soft, wet mouth. By this point, I was intensely turned on, as I felt my panties soak with pleasure. Opening my legs, he slid my dress up, grabbing my thigh as he let out a breath of delight. Reaching down, he began stroking the thin wet material that barely covered my swollen lips. They had plumped up to a pulsing point, as my pussy ached to be touched fully. He rubbed harder as my nails dug into his thigh, and my mouth made little gasps, sucking his penis deeper. He reached up grabbing my ass in frustration as his piercing blue eyes gazed down at my body.

"I need to get you home...now!" He growled, pushing down on the accelerator and careening around a bend. Sitting up to adjust my seat belt, it was exciting to feel the rage of the road below us, as he adeptly controlled the car, while fighting to control his passion.

Passing the garage, Parker screeched to a stop in front of the old English manor house, flinging his door open and hustling to reach mine. Offering his hand, he lifted me out of the car and then wrapped one arm around my waist, and the other around my shoulders, pulling me into a hard kiss. I could feel the bulge of his penis grind against my hips, as I gasped for air. He lifted me, wrapping both my legs around his waist, and pressed me against the front door as he fumbled to place the large ornate iron key into the old lock.

I bit into his shoulder, imploring him to hurry, when I heard the lock turn and the heavy door slowly swing open.

Slamming the door shut with his foot he carried me into the sitting room and set me down on the couch. Straddling my thighs, he pushed my dress up, pulled the thin thong away, and buried his head into my lap. Sucking on my swollen lips like a French kiss, I grabbed his thick black hair and rubbed my clitoris in circles on his lips. The blast of electricity that ran through my body, made me arch in pleasure. Kissing my pussy with three quick pecks, he stood up and said "Don't move! I will be right back". He left the room before I could object, so I moved my fingers down my stomach, reaching to give myself satisfaction. I rubbed the engorged nub in little circles as I felt the wetness build, and that is how he found me, in the throes of self-pleasure. He had brought a large red box with black piping, and to my surprise, it was filled with a bounty of sex toys. Aside from mistakenly stumbling into a sex shop in Times Square in NYC, I had never seen so many toys, and I was very excited to play. "Lay back", he commanded as he pulled a small bullet vibrator from the pile. Putting it on a low speed, he lightly brushed it along my thigh. The sensation ran up my leg, as I realized the power of this little gift. He would kiss my thigh and then stroke it with vibrations, tantalizing me and making me squirm. Gently laying the vibrator on my clitoris, I went momentarily wild, gasping at the shot of pleasure that coursed through me. Staring into his eyes, he chuckled at my wild-eyed disbelief.

"There is so much more to come" he teased, placing the vibrator onto my clitoris once again and sending my spirit straight out of my body. I came so quickly and hard, I began to laugh uncontrollably, a reaction I had learned was standard when I felt out of control, and at this moment, I was completely lost in orgasm. I shook before collapsing against the cushions, limp with pleasure.

Probing me with his eyes, he said "You look so beautiful when you come!"

I smiled in an otherwordly haze as I attempted to catch my breath. Reaching back into the box, he pulled out a gray cock ring and nimbly placed it over his erect dick. Grabbing below my knees he pulled my legs towards him, so my ass sat at the edge of the sofa.

"Are you ready?" he asked teasingly, as I felt my pussy throb. I wanted to be filled and enthusiastically nodded my assent. He pushed a little silver button on the cock ring, and it began to vibrate. His breath sucked in before he plunged his hard cock into my deep folds. The cock ring vibrated against my clitoris as he filled my tight pussy.

The double pleasure sent me into oblivion as I wrapped my arms and legs tighter around him, trying to suck him deeper into my core. Wrapping his arm around me and grabbing my ass, he lifted me off the couch and lowered me to the floor, the full weight of his body on mine, jerking his hips deeper into my vagina. My hands clawed down his back, clutching his butt as his hips bucked in and out. My head tilted back as I gasped for air and then burrowed my mouth against my neck, biting at the skin to hold on as the vibrations lifted me into exciting new territory. Fucking, sucking, vibrating, moaning, biting, licking, each thrust a new sensation as the pleasure within and the pleasure of my clitoris met in a crescendo, and I felt my soul float right out of my body. Ecstasy in duality, my clitoris pulsed, and my pussy tightened around his cock, squeezing every bit, as he screamed in pleasure and his hips pounded the last strokes of orgasm deep inside me. Reaching down he removed the cock ring, turned it off, and flung it aside. Staring down at my naked body, he watched as I twitched, unable to control the orgasmic spasms coursing through me. Laying his body on mine, he kissed my cheeks and nuzzled his face into the crook of my neck.

Breathing deeply, I managed a 'Thank you. That toy is magic!' as my body lay limp underneath him. Nibbling my ear, he teasingly replied "There is so much joy in toys. The pleasure is all mine!"

Skirt Club

I love women; so much so, that my hunt for sensual love and connection led me to join an all women's sex club in New York City. Known as *Skirt Club,* they held private parties in a loft in the east village. This was a members-only club that catered to bisexual and lesbian women, creating a safe space to sexually explore all the female hidden desires, typically overlooked, or shunned in mainstream life. After a brief application process and being granted special acceptance as I was over the standard age limit, I was excited to attend my first event, a soiree held in a penthouse on East Houston Street.

It was raining when the taxi pulled up to the red brick building, and I could see several women at the entrance, waiting to be buzzed in. Rushing to catch up, I joined them as we made our way into an oversized industrial elevator. Staring at each other, I smiled warmly asking if it was their first time. Giggling nervously, they shook their heads in assent to which I responded with "Me too". The comradery broke the awkwardness, as the elevator doors opened to a large hallway with a row of loft size windows. A table, set to the left, was littered with ornate brass keys cinched with burgundy ribbons. Two women dressed in corsets, stockings, and stilettos; one of them holding a tray of bubbly pink champagne flutes beckoned us with their smiles.

"Welcome to the Skirt Club. Please leave your inhibitions at the door" she said in greeting. Laughing at the directive, she checked us in, took our coats, and gifted us each a key. I was dressed in a very low-cut black lace bustier with a neckless of thin gold chains that hung loosely down my chest drawing the eye to a mound of décolletage and further down to lace panties and black stiletto booties. My new acquaintances were dressed in corsets, with fishnet stockings, red bottom heels; hair curled to a voluminous height, and charcoal eye make-up. We were dressed to entice and allure, adding to the sense of playfulness that hung in the air. As we made our way further down the hall, the space opened into a giant loft with a staircase running up the right wall, ending in a large overhanging veranda above us. To the left was a makeshift bar with glass flutes and bottles of rose champagne. Around the room, were women in an array of lingerie and silk finery. It was a modern loft with corset-clad goddesses lounging about. The sight sent shivers through my body as the energy that flowed was one of excitement and enticement. Every one of these women had fantasized about this evening. Together we were a symphony of desire, waiting for permission to be unleashed.

Making my way to the bar, I procured a glass of champagne and offered one to my adopted group. Gazing around the room, we stood in silence, unsure of what to do next.

"Shall we take a tour of the loft? I suggested.

The dual chorus of yes's made us laugh and broke the tension. Turning my attention to the room, I led the way, smiling and raising a mini toast, nodding hello, when I caught someone's eye. We made our way upstairs, wandering in and out of empty walk-in closets, marble bathrooms with whirlpool tubs full of bubbles, and bedrooms laid with silk sheets and body restraints for carnal play. As we surveyed our playground, we also surveyed each other, holding eye contact with those we found interesting.

We made our way back to the landing overlooking the grand room, as a tall, slim brunette decked in a black corset clinked a key against a champagne flute, demanding everyone's attention. Her voice had a posh English accent, and her demeanor displayed that she held herself in high regard.

"Welcome to Skirt Club! My name is Genevieve, and I founded Skirt Club as a space for bi-curious, bisexual, and lesbian women to explore their sexuality and experience female pleasure. We have a few rules that the beautiful Kira will explain momentarily and then I will hand it over to the lovely Penelope who will take you through a brief history of the corset and its role as a symbol of sexuality. After that, you will be free to enjoy each other and explore all the fun ways to connect. I hope you take this opportunity to find joy in your sexuality and in that of the many unique women around you. Let us all be respectful of consent & boundaries; and together let's set the intention to have a beautiful night full of hot, steamy sex!" A sly smile crept across her face, as the group cheered and laughed at her pep talk.

Kira walked us through the safety measures, which set the tone for consensual play, and then Penelope, a red-haired beauty, commanded everyone's attention in an extremely tight corset that left her breasts spilling over the top. Her plump brown nipples, peeked above the compressed material, turning me on immensely. Her full figure was cinched at the waist, making her pale peach-colored ass pop out most deliciously. This was the gift of the corset concept, introduced by Catherine de Medici in France in the 1500s. As Penelope talked about its use in court life and its 400 years of evolution, assistants appeared, modeling the earlier versions of the waist cinch. Some covered the breasts, with peekaboo nipples, while others exposed them for all to see. Worn by both men and women, it had transformed from a way to snatch your waist, to a symbol for sex garments.

Pulling up a chair, Penelope laid a model across her lap and spanked her bottom until a bright pink patch appeared, to which she rubbed and then kissed the spot, adoringly. This act left everyone frozen as a live wire of desire shot through the group. The other models, who had been observing from behind, reached down to rub Penelope's hard nipples, making her moan heavily. Looking up at her guests she said "Please, join us."

I was enthralled by the performance but had my sights on a beautiful dark-haired woman, who was making her way up the stairs. Catching my gaze as she passed by, she let out a little impish grin & wink before heading into one of the large walk-in closets. Turning to my adopted friends, I simply pointed to the door and said "I'll be in there...back in the closet" eliciting more laughs that sent us off in a jovial mood.

Stepping into the darkly lit closet, I could see several other bodies milling about. As the space was the size of the bedrooms, there were plenty of private little wooden cubicles, dimly lit within the room. I slowly walked around the center island, when she stepped out of the shadows, reaching to caress my arm. Looking down at her hand, I leaned in with a silent hello stroking her long thin fingers. She smiled and then pulled me into the dark, her body pressed up against mine. We froze for a moment, as the world around us instantly disappeared, and the only sound was the heavy breaths of anticipation. My excitement grew as her lips nibbled my ear, then sucked on the lobe.

With a sultry whisper, she said "I wanted to kiss your lips, the moment I saw them." Pressing her body against mine, she caught my lips in hers, delicately parting them as her tongue lapped my own. Kissing is an art form when it comes to women; so soft, so sensual, so sexy, and always so sublime. I reached down, rubbing her breast and grabbing an ass cheek. In response, she sought out my clitoris and began rubbing it in circles through the thin silk of my panties. I was weak with pleasure, gasping for air as my legs trembled below me. We were hidden in the recesses of the closet, and the darkness heightened my sense of feeling. Pulling the straps off my bustier, she pulled out my tit, and then I felt the warm sensation of wet mouth and biting teeth against my nipple. As a lover of nipple play, I immediately felt the electric shock travel from my breast down to my vagina, my body humming with pleasure. Sensing my reaction, she pulled aside my panties and dabbed her fingers into my vagina, rubbing the wet outer orifice, as she continued to suck on my nipple. She slowly lowered us to the plush carpet and positioned her body on top of mine, her fingers playing with the swollen nub between my pussy lips. "Are you ready?" She asked, quickening her pace. "Yes" I whispered obligingly as she kissed me again before stuffing three fingers into my tight pussy. Making circular motions, I felt full as the sensations building were driving me to grind my hips, begging to go faster. Gasping for air, she let go of my mouth. Her perk breasts rubbed against my chest as I sought to suck on them. Feeling my desire, she stuffed one in my mouth and continued to finger fuck me. With the pleasure emanating through me, I was lost in her control, as an orgasm shot out, my pussy drowning in wetness, leaving me spasming in the dark. As I came to my senses, my deep breaths inhaled the scent of lavender oil as my face had been buried in her breasts. I could sense her mouth near mine as she asked how I felt. "Orgasmic" I laughed. Realizing that I should reciprocate, I slid my hand down her belly. Grasping it, she said "I think it's time we come out of the closet. There are more adventures and more adventurers". We helped each other to our feet, and she grabbed my hand, leading the way out. As I stepped back onto the landing, I was blinded by the lights. She turned and pulled my hand up to her lips, peppering it with kisses. "Go and enjoy yourself, and I will see you a little bit later," she smiled, before wandering off into the loft.

Realizing I must be in a disheveled state, I made my way to the master bath to freshen up. The door was open and inside a cacophony of howls echoed off the white marble walls.

In the oversize oval tub, two women were cocooned in a mountain of bubbles as they rubbed them up each other's arms, across their shoulders, and down their bare breasts, massaging and laughing. In the shower, three women were lathering a fourth, sensually rubbing their bodies against her as she writhed in pleasure. Upon closer inspection, I could see one was wearing a strap-on and fucking her from behind. The second was squatting on her knees rubbing her clitoris and the third was sucking on her ripe breast. Hands were everywhere, and the sound of their cries sent an echo through the room with each thrust. I could feel my pussy throb at the site of it all, as I ripped my eyes away to look in the mirror. Washing my hands, I fixed my face and readjusted my attire. Abandoning the bustier, I was down to lace underwear and gold chains, my breasts hanging like plump teardrops on either side of the sparkly strands. Staring at the orgy of pleasure through the mirror, I realized I did not care for hard surfaces, and opted to find another room to play in.

Meandering down the hall I found two bedrooms across from each other and decided to turn left. Two women were kissing on the bed, and I stared as the soft satin sheets called to my skin. Rubbing my hands across the silk, one of the women reached over and wrapped her fingers in mine. Pulling me towards them, she smiled and simply said, "I'm Lauren. This is Ellen." "Bex" I smiled and just managed a greeting when Ellen came in for a slow kiss. She had small lips, which seemed to drown in mine. I felt Lauren's hand move up my arm, slowly stroking my skin. Ellen pushed me back onto the bed as Lauren raised my arm and attached it to a cuff that was hanging from the bed corner. Grabbing my other wrist, she locked it in the opposite cuff, as Ellen massaged my breasts and asked if it was okay to blindfold me. I was excited at the suggestion, and replying, "Yes!" she pulled an eye mask from a basket of sex goodies. There was lube, condoms, vibrators, strap-ons, butt plugs, handcuffs, nipple clamps, and much more. A toy chest fit for a master bedroom; I was now wondering what tangled web I had fallen into. As the mask hovered above me, Ellen looked me in the face and said "We just want to please you. Please relax and enjoy. If at any point you want us to stop, just say 'stop'. and then she placed the mask on my face and my world went dark again.

Her hands rubbed my breasts as she tightly pinched my nipple sending my body into a spasm. Two hands began rubbing my thighs, as they massaged me simultaneously. Their touch felt like honey as a sticky heat rose between my legs and I could feel my already wet panties become drenched. The realization that

I had no control excited me, as I felt safe in the situation. The hands on my thighs moved up, as I felt her fingers pull aside the lace, spreading my pussy lips. A warm, wet tongue gently licked the nub between them. The jolt of electricity that shot through my system, made my body tense, as my clitoris pulsed releasing waves of pleasure. The next moment, a mouth was sucking and biting at my nipple, and rubbing my upper body. The wave of pleasure that shot from my nipple to my clitoris was now ricocheting through my body as I writhed beneath them. I was in pure bliss as the sensations felt ever heightened by the removal of my site. Attune to every touch, they continued to play me like an instrument, their mouths sucking, biting, and trilling my clitoris until I cried loudly in orgasm.

Breathing heavily, they pulled away as I felt a little rush of cool wind dance across my exposed frame. Goosebumps formed on my skin, which must have been noticeable as they both proceeded to lay on top of me, each one with half their body over half of mine. I was sandwiched in between them as I felt their warmth, skin to skin. Breasts, arms, hips, and legs laid languidly; I was blissfully floating, when I felt their hips begin to gyrate. Rubbing their vaginas against my upper thighs and hip, I could feel them grind in pleasure. Sandwiched between them, their groans danced around my head like binaural beats, as the sexual energy whipped up into a frenzy. I could feel the friction of their swollen wet pussies as they squirmed in delight. I heard a voice say, "I want to fuck you", and then another voice said, "I want to sit on your face." I thought someone had pushed me off a cliff and I was now in heaven. Her hands reached up, removing my mask, as my lashes fought to pry themselves open. Staring down at me, they waited inquisitively, and I replied with a "yes, please" nodding consent.

Lauren reached over and pulled the strap-on out of the basket, followed by a tube of lube.

Ellen continued to stroke and kiss my breasts, rubbing her soft skin across my frame. I closed my eyes, lost in the hazy folds of pleasure when I felt hands pull my panties off. A dick rubbed up and down, teasing my clitoris between the fatty soft mounds of my inner thighs to rest at the opening to my pussy. I had an ache, a pulsing desire to be pierced, a pain that brought a deep groaning whimper of pleading. Ellen slid up, straddling my head so that her lush pussy lips hung just above my face. Peering through her thighs I could see Lauren hovering between mine, and in one swell motion, they both plunged, smothering my face in pussy and filling my pussy with a large rubber cock. Ellen ground her pussy lips into my mouth as my tongue searched for her clitoris and licked furiously.

The smothered feeling of wet skin was titillating as I felt her hips sway. Lauren was grinding her dick deep in my pussy and I could feel my insides squeezing and releasing with each stroke. Our breasts rubbed against each other, and her hard nipples drew invisible lines of heat across my skin. The pleasure of being face-fucked and pussy fucked as Ellen's cries of "yes, yes, yes" led the pace, I was ridden into another dimension. The explosion of orgasm was an array of feelings that left me weightless and seizing all at once. My body lay frozen in that moment of ecstasy while my mind floated away, among the stars in a blissful state of nothingness. Sensing my orgasm, Ellen slid down and began gently kissing my face and rubbing her chest against mine. Lauren reached into the basket and pulled out a condom. Placing it on the large dick, she proceeded to pull Ellen's ass up so she was bent over doggy style, her knees placed on either side of my hips, and her torso bent over me, so I could

36

see the mounds of her ass cheeks just above her head. Staring into my eyes, I watched the ecstasy bloom across Ellen's face as Lauren pushed the hard cock into her pussy. The sound of wet slapping rang out, as Ellen's hot breathy moans and tight nipples sent me into more desire. The groan of pure pleasure that rang out from her lips made me feel like I was coming all over again, and as the thrusts reached a crescendo, they both tumbled on top of me. We lay there in our orgasmic bubble, all three of us feeling the connection of soft sexual satiation.

Lauren stood up first, unlocking my restraints, and extricating herself from the strap-on.

My body felt heavy as my limbs struggled to pull myself up. Both women came to my aid, helping me stand. "Shall we step outside for some fresh air?" Ellen suggested. I smiled a delirious smile and let them lead me out of the room.

All three of us had left our clothing, and as we stepped out onto the rooftop, the spring air sent a cool breeze across our naked bodies. The rain had ceased, and the light of an almost full moon lit the wooden deck, illuminating several chairs and a large rectangular concrete hot tub, filled with nude women. Some of them were chatting and drinking, while others were in the throes of fingering, kissing, caressing, sucking, and rubbing.

A speaker was blasting Beyoncé's "All Night" as the chorus of enjoyment rang in step with the beat. We were drawn to it, smiling at the beautiful scene of lovemaking. Stepping into the hot tub, the water soothed my indulgently tense muscles. My sigh of pleasure awakened the other women to our arrival, as I watched them each turn to us in greeting, their juicy, plump breasts bobbing above the surface of the water. My eyes lit up and a smile spread across my face, staring at the plethora of delicious tits, glistening in the moonlight. A dark-skinned woman with beautiful full lips and almond-shaped eyes made her way over asking if I would like a massage. "Please", I replied. Suddenly a group of women appeared behind her, and a slew of hands reached out to touch me. Pulling me into the center, they proceeded to lay me flat on my back in the water, my head supported on this strange woman's shoulder as her cheek rubbed against mine. The others began massaging and rubbing my limbs from all angles. A swarm of soft bodies rubbing my shoulders, arms, breasts, ass, pussy, thighs, legs, feet, and face. The feeling was so intense, I could barely breathe as they lifted my orgasm to a place I had never been. Crying out into the night, I sucked in a wild breath of air as my body convulsed, floating in the water, completely lost in ecstasy. My body began to slowly sink as I felt the hands disperse, and the arms around my head reached down to encircle me. I turned to take in her rich ebony skin, water droplets sparkling in the night, and she smiled, pulling me closer to her, wrapping me up in her arms. I tucked my head into the crook of her neck, kissing it, and cupped her breast. My arm wrapped around her, we were entangled in each other's bodies, giving, and receiving what we were both searching for...sensual connection.

The New York Pace

O ne of the keys to achieving orgasm is to find the pace that brings you the most pleasure. In my quest to quench my desires, I had fallen into the 'man pleasing' trap, a mindset that demands performance to hold the male attention. My partner's satisfaction became the end goal, and mine was left wanting. This meant that their pace was the only pace, and if you have ever walked a block in NYC, you know that New Yorkers have one speed: Turbo. This meant that my sexual escapades would devolve into being jack hammered, all sensuous sensations lost. Wanting to get it over with, I would pretend to come, emitting an obnoxious screaming sound, spurring him to join me in the so-called climax.

An overall unsatisfactory experience, and one that seemed to be repeating itself, I was finding it difficult to break the cycle. I knew I needed to pick generous and caring partners, but I was in the cycle of being 'picked' and my lack of assertiveness and boundaries had opened the door to selfish lovers. I was beginning to wonder if this would be my sexual story, a stale tale of unfulfilled fantasies when I had the good fortune of meeting a prominent Radio DJ in New York City. It was 1999 and the world was in a panic over the impending Y2K, a computer glitch that threatened to disrupt or end our modern society. No one was certain what would happen to computers when the new millennium hit, and this uncertainty created an energy that swept through NYC, as everyone had their theory regarding the outcome. Some believed it was nothing, while others thought the modern world we had built would crash, with planes dropping out of the sky the moment the clock struck midnight. No matter their reasoning, there was only one solution: To Party!

I was out one night with a group of girlfriends headed to the hot spot Nell's on West 14th Street. An exclusive nightclub, the doormen were notorious for letting you in one week and then pretending not to know you the next. My girlfriends and I were dressed in the standard NYC club gear: a body-hugging Herve Leger bandage dress, black suede knee-high heeled boots, and a designer clutch. I had straightened my hair, coaled my eyes, and knew we looked good enough to enter, and yet still we waited out front; a hefty bouncer and a red velvet rope blocking our passage. The key is to wait nonchalantly, acting as if you belong, and try your best to catch the bouncer's eye. They will ignore you...until they don't, and your place is to wait.

Standing patiently, I felt someone brush up behind me. Turning to investigate, I came face to face with a chest. Startled, my eyes slowly shifted up until my head followed suit. His height surprised me and I reacted with a bumbling "Oh! Excuse me. Sorry"

"Nothing to be sorry for" he replied, locking eyes for a beat before the bouncer yelled "Slim! What's up, ma man!"

Everyone at the door knew this slender giant, as he greeted them with elaborate handshakes, pats on the back, and half hugs! The bouncer asked if he was alone, and without skipping a beat he pointed in our direction and said, "She's with me".

Standing at attention, I whipped out my most dazzling smile, happy to finally make an entrance. He stretched out his arm, beckoning me to take it, and I obligingly let him shepherd us into the dark.

The club was packed, Fat Joe screaming *'Still not a player'* pumped through the speakers, and I was ever more grateful for this giant to lead the way. With my head down, I had no idea where we were headed, but I somehow knew we were in good hands. He gripped mine tighter, ensuring I didn't get sucked into the crowd, when it suddenly opened to a VIP section. A gentleman who looked like he could have been in a Bad Boy rap video was entertaining an entourage of beautiful women. Flanked by video vixens, he was decked in all white with a matching Kangol bucket hat, and he beamed in excitement at the sight of us. We exchanged quick intros, too loud to hear, our voices swept away by a 'Tribe called quest.' A bottle waitress poured Grey Goose & sodas, which 'slender' graciously passed to each one of us. Our host made room on the banquet, and I made sure to situate myself on the end, next to our giant. My heels dug into the leather seat, and as I sought to find my balance, his arm reached around to hold me steady. At this height, we were almost eye to eye, and I leaned in to ask his name once again. Known publicly as 'Slim', he was a hip hop DJ with his own radio show on hot95, a famous NY station. Standing at 6'6, his height matched his status, with a large, narrow head that complimented his lanky stature. His hair was already graying with random streaks of white, making him stand out in a nightclub, like a lone glowing candle in the dark. He knew every word to every song, and together we rapped in unison caught up in our private show. Drinking, laughing, dancing, and spitting rhymes, the energy we weaved drew us closer together. Making eye contact, he leaned in; his large, plush lips enveloping mine with a soft, slow, sensual kiss that sent heat coursing through my body. Finally pulling away, we were both surprised by the magnetism that sparked between us. Time seemed to stand still, and all the sounds of the club disappeared as if we were in a vacuum. I was holding my breath, finally inhaling deeply as all the sounds came rushing back around me. Suddenly the space felt too cramped and hot, as bodies writhed to the music.

Fanning myself with my hand he placed his cold glass of ice on the back of my neck. I smiled and thanked him, feeling his hand massage mine, soothing the tension. Leaning in he said, "Let's get out of here!" I nodded in agreement and turned to let my crew in on the plan. As if they had known what was coming, Sha Sha lifted her hand to wave goodbye yelling "Have fun! Don't get knocked up!"

Once again leading me through the crowd of drunk club kids, the simple act of holding my hand gave me a sense of calm amongst all the chaos. We spilled out onto the street, and he raised his hand to hail a cab, turning to me to ask, "My place?" I squeezed his hand replying "Sure".

The cab ride back to his place in Tribeca was heated, our hands groping and caressing, our lips kissing and searching to taste every bit of exposed skin. Once again lost in our world, the driver had to cough loudly when he pulled up to the building to let us know we had arrived.

We walked two flights up an old narrow wooden staircase, which momentarily made me second-guess my choices.

Opening the door to a spacious loft, I was mesmerized by the wall of vinyl records that spanned the length of the entire space. Bookshelves stacked from floor to ceiling with one of the greatest private collections of music I had ever seen. Buttressed on each side of the loft were floor-to-ceiling windows, the front window framing a DJ deck with turntables, massive speakers, and an array of equipment.

"Make yourself at home." He said warmly. "You want a beer?"

"Sure. And water please" I responded, kicking off my boots. Wandering the stacks of vinyl, I pulled out random records, his music spanning genres and decades. Turning to him as he passed me a beer, I said "Can you guess, the first record I ever owned?

I will give you a hint. The woman on the cover is wearing leg warmers."

The laugh that shot out of him was so cute, it was contagious, and I giggled a little. He walked down the length of the wall, his fingers lightly brushing across the thin spines of the sleeves, stopping to pull out a record. I started laughing and clapping as he held up the album to the Movie FlashDance. I jokingly busted out a move, belting the chorus to "What a feeling!". Once again, he joined in, singing in unison, and I was enamored with his knowledge of music. I always had a song in my head and my empathic ability to feel meant that music would move me to the deepest wells of emotion. Pulling out another album, he deftly placed the record on the turntable and set the needle at a specific spot. The rich sounds of Marvin Gay crooning "Let's get it on" played over the speakers.

"Oh! How original." I teased as he threw me a wink. "Do you know what is so funny and made me realize that maybe I wasn't that smart of a kid?"

He tilted his head curiously. "You want to share something stupid about yourself?"

"Yes, exactly that!". I replied, both of us laughing.

"No, please. Go right ahead. What was funny?" He asked in a mock 'serious' tone, which made me laugh even more.

Swigging my beer I replied, "Do you remember the singer Olivia Newton John?"

"Yes! Who could forget? More leg warmers! I'm noticing a theme here." He said, emphasizing the forget.

"Yes!" I giggled. "Her song? 'Let's get physical' I was 22 years old when I heard that song as an adult and realized it was about sex. I believed it was just a workout song. I was standing in the middle of CVS thinking 'Oh my god! This is about sex.' Stupid, I know!" I said shyly. He laughed even harder, pulling me closer and wrapping his long arms around my body.

"I don't think you were stupid at all. I think it is sweet. It means your childhood was innocent." he replied. Smiling up at him, he leaned down and gave me a long, sensual kiss. He was caressing my back and drawing patterns into the skin, a meditative movement that made my body fall into his. Pulling me over to the other side of the loft, a giant wood-framed bed with a silken white California King comforter took up most of the space. At 6'6, he required a specially made bed, and as a lover of pure comfort, it looked like a sea of softness. He unzipped my dress, kissing down my neck, peeling the tight layers off to reveal golden brown skin. My panties dropped to the floor, and I stood in all my nakedness. He stared at me slowly, taking in the soft curves of my breasts and hips, and subtle color changes in my skin, as if building a mental map of my physique.

"You are stunning!" He spoke. The words were hanging between us as I tried to calm my self-conscious thoughts. As a model and actress, my body had been picked apart in castings and dress fittings, making me hypersensitive to people's opinions. At least in castings, I had the excuse that I just was not the type they were locking for. In real life, the fear was that someone might not like what they see. In reaction to this feeling, I stepped backward and star-fished across the bed on my back.

Laying smack in the middle of this plush pool of bedding, I giggled and writhed as the soft sheets caressed my even softer skin. His eyes were ablaze, and he stripped off his clothes, my mind pretending to unwrap him like a gift. Peeling off his boxer briefs, his penis was in perfect proportion to his giant frame, large, long, and lanky. He reached down and began to stroke his cock, coaxing the length to fill and bulge until the head glistened, ready to burst. I reached down and stroked my clitoris, making my favorite circular motions staring at him. We watched each other, eyes locked, stroking ourselves as all manner of pleasure morphed across our faces. When he could no longer take it, he bound into bed, laying his giant frame over mine, my legs wrapping around his hips, welcoming him in. The hunger building, my pussy ached to be filled by this beautiful cock, and he rubbed it against my swollen outer lips, teasing me to even more wetness. Wrapping himself in a condom, he looked into my eyes and asked "Yes?"

I smiled and nodded quickly with a definitive "Yes!".

He slowly pushed his penis into my sopping wet pussy, letting me get used to the size and breath of him. We were laying prone, face to face, and with slow and very deliberate movements he began to stroke in and out. The sensations blew my spirit away, as ripples and ripples of pure pleasure wafted through me. His measured pace let me feel every inch of him, and I groaned at the sheer delight of it all. Time was endless as I writhed in this sea of slithering limbs, every cell screaming in gratification.

His lips, fat from kissing, sucked and bit my own. His large hands grasped mine, guiding them above my head, my body stretched out, my mind floating in the ether of joy. The pace was long and drawn out, insisting I enjoy each inch of him, and sending my mind into another world. He began to quicken, as I squirmed in delight, driving towards completion, when suddenly he slowed it down again, moving in time with the music. His hips swung in circles, as he was fucking me to the melody, and the feel of his skin sliding across mine sent me deeper into ecstasy. I was pinned under him, and the thrill of it sent me to new heights. A deep sigh breached my lips, as the sensation exploded through me, the experience pulling me into a state of surprise and laughter. The sound of giggling increased with each wave of orgasm that continued to spill over me. It was as if I was having energy currents of pleasure bursting through my body, a new and tantalizing experience. He rolled over laying on his back, next to me. Staring at my giggling face, he asked "Are you alright?"

"I'm fucking amazing!" I replied, my eyes wide with delight and my body laughing in rejuvenation. "I'm saved!"

He began to laugh with me, joy emanating between us. The sound faded away as we caught our breaths, staring at each other.

"Thank you!" I said, ever grateful for the orgasm. "You don't know it, but you saved me."

"Well, I'm glad you recognize it is God, Jesus, and then me doing the heavy work of saving." He replied, pulling me close as we giggled and held each other in the afterglow of orgasm.

Scissor Sirens

malia! Amalia! Amalia! The most beautiful woman I had the pleasure of being with was an actress, whose energy was both sultry and serene. She had dark brown hair, sun-kissed skin with golden undertones and her dimpled smile was both cute and stunning. She was introduced to me by Arthur, a fellow actor who was fresh off the media tour of a famous Colombian drug show. He invited me for drinks and mentioned that his co-star and a few friends would be joining us. He believed we would hit it off, and after meeting Amalia, I knew he was right.

Our first introduction was at a restaurant in Silver Lake in Los Angeles. The dark wood bar ran the length of the venue leading to an outdoor back patio, filled with candle-lit tables, and dark green ivy walls. The melody of an old Spanish love song lulled the atmosphere into reverie, as the last glow of L.A.'s hazy deep red sunset disappeared from the sky. Amalia was sitting at a table, conversing with several other actors when we arrived. Upon looking at each other, I could sense our mutual attraction as she stood to be introduced. Her mid-length hair was pulled up into a loose top knot with tendrils that fell softly around her face. Sultry Brown eyes beamed at me from behind long dark lashes, and the pink pout of her bow-shaped lips spread into a beaming smile as we hugged in greeting.

"Please, sit next to me," she said and pulled the chair out beside her. Arthur kicked off the conversation, telling stories of their onset experiences and off-set escapades which had included a threesome with a Colombian dancer they had met on a night out. Listening as they recounted the incredible sexual adventure; my imagination was piqued.

It was Amalia's first experience with a woman, and Art was salivating at the memory. I was a little apprehensive at his reaction, as I had always kept my relationships with women separate from that of men. In my experience, the men I dated did not know how to behave once they heard the term bisexual. Their porn hub fantasies had led them to believe that they would be the center of attention in a threesome, and when I explained that would never happen, they resorted to negotiating a third option; to watch. Having no desire for performative sex, I turned my attention back to Amalia, taking in the heart-shaped lines that crafted her face. She seemed to glow from within, and I found myself staring uncontrollably. The energy was a mix of laughter, sexual tension, and nerves; a giddy teenager talking to her first crush. Everyone at the table noticed as well, and as Arthur excused himself to use the bathroom he said "I was right about you two. There is something exquisite brewing. Please, just let me watch, please!!" We laughed at his desperate plea and then turned back to our private huddle. He was right though, and staring at each other in that moment, we both knew it. She smiled that dimpled smile and leaned in whispering, "I have some good weed. Do you smoke?"

"Definitely!" I chuckled, tickled by her conspiratorial tone. Taking my hand, she led me to an area of the garden that was slightly obscured by overhanging vines. Pulling out her vape, she took a hit and passed it to me. I took a long pull on the weed pen, breathing deeply, an immediate hit of THC rushing to my brain.

"Holy shit, that's fucking good!" I blurted out.

The beautiful sound of her laughter rang through the night, and I could not help but join in, eventually evolving into mutual giggles.

"You are so cute!" She said, shaking her head.

"I can say the same of you." I teased in return, passing the vape back and forth again. Taking two more puffs, my head floated off my body, a giant smile permanently stuck to my face.

"Are you good?" she asked, holding up the pen.

"I honestly have never felt better. There is something about your energy and your spirit that is drawing me to you." I admitted. My brain had melted, and my tongue was loose, as the weed drew out my vulnerabilities. Our eyes locked, and she leaned in slowly, her gorgeous little plump lips brushing against my cheek. She made a trail of little kisses down my face, and I turned my head to greet her lips. The softness and sensuality felt like she was exploring my spirit as our energies co-mingled.

My hands reached around to explore her back, and I marveled at how small she felt in my arms. Although she initiated the kiss, I suddenly felt a rush of protectiveness. I had to stop myself from asserting dominance and coaxed my mind to simply enjoy the moment rather than steer or control it. It was too easy to fall into the roles played by standard gender norms, and I wanted my experience with this woman to be real.

Realizing I was overthinking, I forced my mind to the present, allowing the sensations of her tongue to pull me deeper into the heated haze. Her breasts teasing my chest, forced me to pull away, my desire wanting to cup them, but my mind knowing we could only go so far in public.

Staring at each other hungrily, she leaned in again planting a quick peck, and said, "Let's go back to mine." I nodded yes, as my lips seemed unable to form words, a whimsical smile stuck permanently to my face.

Our return to the table was met with a chorus of "Ooh La La's. Where have you two been and what have you been doing?!!"

Flashing a sly grin, Amalia replied "None of your business! We're off. Te quiero mucho!"

Peppering us with farewell kisses, Art gushed at his handy work, lamenting his early morning flight as the reason he would not be joining the late-night festivities.

We took an Uber to Amalia's place and sat like two teenagers in the back seat of their parents' car getting a ride home after a date. Caressing each other's hands, playing with the stirring sensations running through the skin, we both knew we had to be covert. Our concerns revolved around the unwanted attention displayed by men who see two women as objects of ownership; and Amalia's recent Hollywood work had relegated her to sex symbol status, a persona she now needed to uphold.

Stepping out of the car, we both felt the connection surge, and she grabbed my hand pulling me up the stairs into her place. Her petite fingers felt soft and strong, and I wanted them all over my body. Dropping her purse, she turned to me, smiling, and began to remove her top. My eyes lit up as her breasts spilled over the top of her push-up bra. Luring me to her, she moved backward towards the bedroom, slowly removing her skintight jeans. Mesmerized by the sway of her body and the curve of her hips, I could not pull my eyes away, my body floating towards hers as if I was locked in her tractor beam. Standing before me in a purple bra and panties, I wanted to devour her.

Stepping up, I caressed her arms, taking her hands and pulling her closer. Our lips met in a surge of sexual heat, my hands reaching around to unfasten her bra. Slowly removing it, she let it fall to the floor, her golden cream skin spread across perky breasts that framed chestnut brown nipples.

Cradling her body, I bent down licking them until they hardened, and a little whimper slipped from her lips. The sound spurred me on, as I rubbed her other breast, pinching until I heard another whimper. Kissing down her belly, I stripped off her panties, kneeling before her exposed body.

"You are glorious!" I whispered. "So stunning and beautiful and funny and...." The words trailed away as I felt a wave of emotion come over me.

She smiled, her beautiful energy bathing me in the glow of her happiness. Leaning in, I kissed the soft skin at the crease of her thigh and then licked it. Making my way inwards, my lips slowly kissing and licking, discovering the little landing strip of hair that ran down the middle of her vagina leading my mouth to her clitoris. Nuzzling it with my nose, I rubbed my face around the soft skin before wrapping my lips around it to seek her clitoris. My tongue peeled apart the satin folds of skin, licking the fat nub that engorged itself with pleasure. I heard a sharp intake of breath as I began to tease and suck, her hands reaching down to grip my hair and grinding her hips into my mouth. Cupping her ass cheeks, I quickened my pace, flicking my tongue over and over, sending her body into little convulsions; her cute little moans piercing the quiet room.

Holding my head tightly, she steered her hips until a sweet cry of orgasm rang out, her pussy wet with gratification.

Pulling me over to the bed she reached down and pulled my dress up over my head. Adorned only in underwear, she stared, her eyes growing wide as they took in my naked form. "Has anyone ever told you, you should be a model?" She smiled.

"Thank you for the compliment!" I responded with a laugh. "Many, many years ago, I was one."

Extending her hand, she pulled at the thin straps of my panties, removing them completely. Her soft hands rubbed my thighs, up my hips, and across my stomach. "You have the softest skin. I have never felt anything as soft" she commented in awe. Pulling me towards her onto the bed, our bodies touched, the skin igniting as I held my breath. Rubbing her body against mine, the sensation was overwhelming, and I felt myself falling into her universe. The feel of her lips, breasts, skin, and ass rubbing against me, as we writhed together. Sliding her leg between my thighs, I rubbed my clit against her and felt her wet pussy rub against mine. This mutual exchange of friction sent us into a tizzy as we continued our fevered caresses, both of us yearning for more pleasure. I was lost in the smooth supple lines of her soft skin, her lips sucking on mine, and her wet pussy rubbing and grinding against me. I moaned, the pace quickening, our bodies dancing and scissoring. A rush of feelings wafted over me, as a crescendo of orgasm ripped through my body, our legs locked together as one. Panting with exertion, we lay in each other's arms, the haze of satiation making our muscles relax. She was beaming, and her beautiful energy made me pull her closer into a tight cuddle. Stroking her back, we lay together in bliss. Lifting her head, she looked me in the eyes once again and asked, "Does this make us scissor sisters?"

The laugh that erupted came from deep within me, and I

rolled over onto my back, my breasts shaking with amusement. She rubbed a circle around my nipple, and cupped it, squeezing gently.

"That was scissoring, but the 'sisters' part is a bit iffy. I think we need to reframe that, don't you?" I asked teasingly.

"Yes! How about Scissor sirens?" She asked, kissing my shoulder.

"I like it. You are seductive and tempting. Scissor sirens it is!" I announced, kissing her gently on the lips.

We held each other, basking in the afterglow of orgasm, laughter, and connection, before slowly drifting off to sleep.

Positions of Lust

Flexibility is an advantage in the bedroom if your goal is to increase pleasure, and as a former gymnast, I was in awe of the acrobatic dance of lust. I use the word 'lust', because that was the place I had found myself, when I started a relationship with a young doctor from Puerto Rico, twenty years my junior. He had approached me on the street, asking for my number and the opportunity to take me out. Having recently exited a ten-year relationship, the thought of dating or even kissing someone else was anxiety-inducing. Asking his age, he informed me he was 25, to which I replied that I was 45, believing I had the perfect excuse to listen to my fears and turn him down.

Fortunately, this did not deter him, and after a little coaxing, I agreed to see him.

After an entertaining first date over sushi and sake, I was still struggling with the idea of being with someone new, but that all changed with our first kiss. Standing out front of my apartment building, we faced each other in that moment of awkwardness after an evening out. I had guarded my emotions, weary of letting new people into my life after a long and tumultuous breakup. Having chosen to retreat into myself to heal, this was the first time I would let my guard down, and the nerves made me uncomfortable. He leaned in and stroked my cheek, tilting my head up to meet his gaze. I froze and then his lips touched mine and it felt like a hot coal searing my lips.

The fire spread across my face, down my neck, and into my chest as I began to melt into him. Reaching his arm around my body, he sucked my tongue deeper into my mouth and squeezed my ass. The awakening of dormant desire ripped through my body, as I felt my passion unleashed. With that one kiss, he flipped the switch, and I felt like myself again. My desire, no longer suppressed by depression and loss, bloomed. I felt an awakening, understanding that my need for love, sex, touch, and connection would always be a guiding force in my life.

I had opted to wait before sleeping with him, instituting the third date rule, asking myself the same questions over and over: "Is he worthy of me? Is he worthy of this body?" It was not an easy task, as he had awakened my desire and I wanted more. My inner monologue continued to struggle with the array of new dating issues:

"Why can't I just sleep with him? Men do it all the time. He's 25. He is way too young. Is there any kind of future for us? Do I even want something serious?" All the while fantasizing about touching him, this anticipation exposed a deep hunger that led us to a frenzied third date. We had been partying at a small underground club in the lower east side, and between the tequila shots and grinding dance moves, our sexual appetites were ravenous.

Stumbling back to my apartment, he pulled me into a kiss as we waited for the elevator to ascend. Spilling into my place, we hurriedly pulled each other's clothes off, fumbling to touch, kiss, rub, and devour. At six feet, he was tall, but with a stocky build. Skin the color of cafe au lait, he was hairless from the neck down to his ass, his stubbled muscular legs being the only exception. Picking me up and wrapping my legs around his waist he carried me into the bedroom, our lips never ceasing to part.

His style of lovemaking was filled with passion, pleasure, and positions. Laying me across the king-size bed, he began by taking pleasure in eating me out.

My legs spread eagle across the bed as my fingers clutched his perfectly cut, coarse brown hair, laid between my thighs, his mouth sucking my clitoris sending my pussy into wet spasms. Kissing my belly, stopping only to suck on my perky tits, he pushed his erect penis into my wet pussy, then caught my lips as they moaned in pleasure. It felt like he was stealing my soul as he devoured my mouth and ground his hips into mine. The standard missionary was more than standard, as I felt the heat of our bodies and the fullness of his penis press itself deeper and deeper into my core.

One leg up!
One leg down!
Both legs up!
Flip me around!

He would change positions, and I would find myself sitting cowgirl, riding his beautiful cock. The next moment I was ass up, head down, bent over in doggy style. Each transition from position to position done effortlessly, as our bodies morphed together in an erotic dance.

Reaching down, he pulled both my legs up over my head and wrapped his arms under my bent knees. "Grab my neck", he whispered. I did as he commanded, and was shocked as he lifted me, standing upright, sliding his penis even deeper. Staring into my eyes, he slowly began to lift and lower, as I found myself impaled on his hard cock, hitting my g-spot perfectly. My eyes went wide with pleasure, as this was a new position that brought waves of new feelings. I felt stars shooting up my body, as he built the pace, keeping his eyes locked on my face. The pleasure and excitement made my face warp, and my heart raced as my breath whipped in and out and a loud moan erupted from somewhere deep inside me. Ripples of ecstasy coursed through my legs, as my body felt like it had imploded, and I was once again a shooting star floating in the nebulous regions of space.

Time did not exist between us as he pumped hard to climax, and his legs shook in the aftermath. Laying me down on the bed, his body spasmed, as he lowered my legs and wrapped me in his arms. I brushed back his hair and kissed his face, basking in the warm glow of sex.

Rolling onto our side, he kept his penis locked in my pussy, never ceasing to let me go. We lay panting, trying to catch our breath. As the air danced swiftly in and out, we found our rhythm, until we were fully synced as one. With a beaming smile, I lay in the glow of our ecstasy. He stared, a well of emotions alighting his face. I felt a deep fondness, our emotions encapsulating us in our joyous world. A beautiful place, with unspoken expressions of desire, lost in the embrace of lust. To feel the orgasm writhing in every cell of your body that there is no place for it to go, but to shine on the person who brought joy back into your life.

Eyes locked, drifting in our bubble, he gently caressed my face and said "You are so beautiful. Be with me." This proclamation sent a wave of emotion, the desire erupting once again. Pulling his face closer, I kissed his lips with a passionate sensuality that set his cock thrumming inside of me. I was overjoyed by his stamina, and rolled us over, sitting cowgirl style on his dick. Clutching his chest, I began to move my hips forward and back, grinding ever deeper, as I searched to hit that cosmic spot. My clitoris rubbing against his skin, at just the right angle, my pussy explodes in wetness, drenching his balls and emitting little sucking noises. His eyes widened in ecstasy with each pump of my hips, as deep grunting sounds emerged from his lips. I was in control now, and I wanted to bring him as much pleasure as he had given me. Grinding and riding, I teased him to the edge of orgasm, before pulling out and turning around to ride him in reverse. He wasn't prepared for the wave of sensation that hit him when I brought the weight of my pussy down to envelope his dick, once again. In 'reverse cowgirl', I could feel his hard cock rubbing the back wall of my pussy sending ripples of enjoyment up my spine. Reaching for my vibrator, I deftly placed it between my legs and continued my race to orgasm. The buzz buzzing hit my clit, making my pussy clench tighter around his dick, as my body shot into double orgasm. Loving the sensation, I furiously rode his cock, completely out of control, a loud, drawn-out scream bursting from his lips as he jutted them in time with my orgasm. My body felt as though it was released from the past, and I flopped over onto the bed, sweaty and exhausted from my ride, a wild and satisfied smile on my face. He reached over, pulling back the wet strands of hair that had clung to my forehead. I peered down at his cock which was still hard. Looking at him curiously he winked and said, "Round two?"

I laughed, smiling mischievously, my body limp and slack from the exertion. "Abso-fucking-lutely!"

Prone Bone Pandemic

Have you ever fallen in love with a position, and found that all you ever want is to be fucked in that position? That was my predicament when I met the Spaniard, whose penis was so perfect for prone bone, I was constantly trying to 'assume the position'.

It was 2020, at the height of the COVID pandemic in New York City and most New Yorker's had spent their time cooped up in tiny apartments losing their already fragile minds.

We had been in lock down for several months, and it was incredibly difficult to date when there were no public spaces to meet people. This drove me online to *Hinge*, a common dating app that many of my friends had found to be successful. Crafting a 'come hither' profile, I immediately matched with a slew of men and women. It seems I was not the only one who was bored and in need of a good fucking before the world officially ended. The Spaniard's profile was cute, as he worked in marketing, and from his photos, I could tell he had the heart of an artist. Set among the backdrop of beaches, bicycles, and beautiful sketches, he stood with a lean, wiry frame, oil black curls, an elongated bearded face, and a sharp nose that he held aloft as if sniffing for something in the winds.

After chatting for a few days, we agreed to meet up for drinks in the park, the outdoors being the only spaces available to safely congregate. He was standing in front of a bar on the Williamsburg waterfront that had opened a window out to the world to sell cocktails 'to go'. I approached him and smiled as I saw that he was better looking in person than in profile, a rarity when online dating. Standing at 5'11 he had the slim muscular build of a cyclist. Introducing myself, he stepped forward to hug me, bringing with him a waft of sandalwood oil. The scent took me back to my days in Turkey, sniffing the heavily fragrant oil pots at the Grand Bazaar. I was immediately calmed by his presence and for the first time, amid pandemic madness, I felt at peace. Mirroring his energy, we spent the afternoon sipping cocktails by the waterfront, commenting on the mish-mosh of characters that had emerged from their tiny NYC apartments, ravenously soaking up the sun. He had a gentle and creative nature, having spent his lock down learning to sketch and perfecting the art of Japanese cuisine; unlike myself, who had made doom scrolling my new addiction. His kindness led me to agree to dinner at his apartment, and after learning of all the delicious dishes he planned to prepare, I was hooked. Fortunately for him, I was easily tempted by words like *Omakase* and *Usuzukuri*. Bemoaning his attempts to perfect *tamagoyaki*, the Japanese omelet, had me salivating at thoughts of breakfast in bed, and like a kid offered candy, I was off to his place.

His industrial-style apartment was lined with tall windows and adorned with a slew of exotic plants; the indoor garden a beautiful respite from the concrete jungle of Brooklyn and the suffocating air of an over-polluted city. Filling my lungs, time seemed to stand still, and as I perused his collection of bicycles,

I felt a new sense of anticipation at the thought of his stamina.

Pouring us a glass of sake, the Spaniard put on some music and then got to work creating our dinner. I sat on a stool at the kitchen bar, overseeing his progress and making a running commentary of his movements as if he were on *Hell's Kitchen* and I was his personal Gordon Ramsey.

"You call this a julienne carrot? Your knife skills are *shite!*" I teased, as he laughed at my faux English accent. "Just kidding!" I said, peering over his shoulder. "Are you making *chirashi*? That's incredible." I gushed, excited to have a Japanese meal without the exorbitant price tag. It had been a while since I dined out, and as I watched his hands deftly chop, slice, season, and spice, my heart was tickled at being served. In the past, I would have put the maximum effort into designing a meal in the hopes of gaining a partner's love or attention. During the pandemic, I found that I no longer cared, but I was in awe of the effort he put in for me.

"Thank you for making me dinner. This is so kind and so sweet." I added, my gratitude beaming from the corners of my smile.

"The pleasure is all mine! I love that you know what I am making." He replied.

"I love Japanese food. It's one of my favorite cuisines." I shared.

Turning to face me, we stood staring, a Spaniard and an African, both bonding over their love of Japanese food. I could feel our energies begin to link and pull at each other. He smiled and then nervously turned his attention back to slicing the raw fish. I sat back down at the kitchen bar, watching his every move, and sipping my cold sake. Catching my eye again, he fumbled, dropping a pan on the floor, and a bright red shade spread across his face.

"Do I make you nervous?" I asked, smiling to put him at ease.

"Maybe a little. I mean obviously." He replied, dipping down to pick up the wayward pan.

"Why?" I pressured.

He took a moment to collect himself and answered "Because you are so beautiful. You are. You are one of the most beautiful women I have ever seen, and you are sitting in my kitchen. How did I get so lucky?"

Now I was the one blushing. The compliment made me smile from ear to ear, as I raised my glass, toasting in Japanese. "Thank you. *Kanpai!*"

Clinking glasses he asked if I was ready to eat.

By now, the sake had taken effect and I was starving for more than just a meal.

The table was laid with an array of gorgeous delicacies, my favorite being the tuna *tostadas* with avocado, a dish I had once enjoyed at the famous restaurant, *Contramar* in Mexico City. A fusion of Spanish and Japanese flavors, the Asian zucchini slaw, and the assortment of seasoned raw fish and vegetables on a bed of sushi rice made my spirit sing. His mastery of these delicate and savory dishes made me want him even more.

This was a man who delighted in creating, and his appreciation for craft and beauty was a turn-on. Staring at him a little too hard, he blushed, and asked 'What? Why are you staring at me?"

"I just can't believe you made this. It's exceptional. Which makes you exceptional," I complimented.

"Ah no. I just cooked dinner. You are giving me way too much credit" he replied.

"I'm just trying to figure out how I can spoil you in return." I laughed flirtatiously.

"Ah mi bonita! You are making me sweat!" He laughed, reaching over to place his hand on mine.

"No, but really. Thank you. This was such a treat." I said as I took his hand. We played with each other's fingers, caressing, and touching, staring with big smiles on our faces. Spanish music played in the background, the staccato strums of a guitar stealing our attention. He stood, pulling my hand up to his mouth and placed a kiss.

"Mi Bonita! May I have this dance?"

I stood and let him lead me to the middle of the room, pulling me into his body and wrapping his arms in a dancer's embrace. We swayed slowly to the beat, my head resting in the crook of his neck. I breathed in the scent of him, the pheromones lighting up the pleasure centers in my brain. I moved my hands across his back, rubbing his muscles, so pleased to touch and be touched. It was as if our bodies were saying "Hello, nice to meet you, I like how you feel."

Leaning down, he kissed my forehead, a motion that seemed too intimate for first-time lovers, but my body responded, craving it. Continuing to kiss down my cheek, I moved my mouth to meet his, the heat rising between us. He took my lip in his and sucked it gently, pulling me deeper into him. The kiss was slow and seductive, and we took our time enjoying each sensation as we had enjoyed our meal. Coming up for air, he smiled down at me, as we continued to sway. Placing his hands on my back he began massaging my shoulders and neck. It felt like heaven as my legs swayed with exhaustion.

"Would you like a massage?" He offered. I laughed knowing full well a massage is 'couple code' for foreplay. I was happy to consent, considering an orgasm is not always guaranteed, so at least I would get a massage out of it. Slowly dancing our way into the bedroom, I was surprised to find a traditional Japanese platform bed, the white sheets contrasting with the dark wood grain, giving it the effect of floating.

I stripped off my clothes, unabashedly lying face down, naked on the bed, and he hurried to follow. Pulling a bottle of coconut oil from the shelf, he straddled my hips and began rubbing the oil into my back. Brushing circles down my spine he did not hesitate to knead my juicy round ass, his hands kissing, rubbing, and molding the mounds of rich brown skin. The tension in my muscles eased, as the fire inside began to build. Stroking and kissing and rubbing up my body, his semi-hard dick pushed between my ass cheeks, and I could feel it rub back and forth as he stroked my back. His balls splayed against my thighs, and his cock grew harder and longer the more he rubbed. I responded by grinding my hips slowly into him, making sure my ass cheeks stroked the length of his cock. Turning my head, he leaned down and kissed me, rubbing his body against my back, the sensation making me squirm in pleasure. I reached down and began playing with my clitoris, my hips continuing to grind. Driving him mad, he pulled a condom from the bedside table and quickly put it on. Laying prone on my belly, I raised my ass, and he slid his hard cock into my pussy. The feel of his skin on my back, as he lay on me, pushing his dick deeper was absolute heaven. The love language of physical touch coupled with doggy style, meant that prone bone was the perfect position and allowed me the most skin-to-skin contact while hitting that ideal spot you can only reach from behind.

This position required just the right shape and size for maximum pleasure, and thankfully the Spaniard was packing. With a slow grind, his hips bucked back and forth, smashing my ass cheeks down to reach deeper into my pussy. I could feel the length of his penis sliding in and out, as he reached around grabbing my breast with one hand and lifting my chin with the other. His lips brushed against my cheek before opening and sucking my neck, my soul moaning at the sensation. The heat of our skin grew slick, our bodies sliding in one fluid motion, the scent of warm coconut oil mingled with sweat. Continuing to strum my pussy, I felt my body lifting as his cock pumped, his fingers squeezed my nipple, and his skin pressed tightly to mine. Once again I was being played like an instrument, and the Spaniard was an excellent 'cellist'. Our bodies gyrating and grinding, the pleasure rising to a boil, I felt weightless as if I was at the top of a roller coaster floating in blissful clouds. A loud guttural sound exploded next to my ear as his ejaculation brought me back to earth and I sped up my motions, grinding his dick deeper to reach my satisfaction. Engulfing my body, we lay panting, lost in the mess of orgasm, our wet limbs shiny from exertion. His mop of black curls stuck to his forehead, and as I gently wiped the sweat from his brow he grasped my hand, kissing it tenderly saying "In the middle of a pandemic, I found you. How am I so lucky?"

I smiled impishly in response, happy to finally find the perfect 'prone bone' pandemic partner!

Spring in Paris

I t has always been a fancy of mine to experience Paris in love...or at least, in lust! With such high expectations, I had worried over the years that a Parisian romance would be a disappointment and had refused to visit until I was certain I had chosen the right companion. These types of adventures had been over-dramatized in tacky films, and I wanted the real experience filled with the beauties and blunders of a dirty French tryst.

The journey into my sexual awakening was inspired by the Parisian author Anais Nin, so it was not lost on me that my desire to truly experience Paris must live up to the lust and desire of *Erotica*.

Luckily for me, the summer prior, I had been introduced to Malik Serer, a Senegalese gentleman whose skin was as dark as pitch black night that glistened with a red richness in its' undertones. He was a businessman, whose home base was South Africa, but he spent his week making deals across the African continent. Our last meeting had ended in a whirlwind threesome, and we had stayed in touch, musing over once again feeding our sexual appetites. Although threesomes are delightful, we both wanted to explore each other solo, so he initiated a plan to meet in Cape Town, South Africa, where we would spend a week relaxing at a beautiful vineyard in Stellenbosch. Face timing to update me, he dropped the sweetest little bomb. He had to meet with his bankers in Paris and asked if I would be okay joining him for five days in the most romantic city in Europe before we made our way to the Southern Hemisphere. I was tickled, as the teenager in me began dreaming of spring in Paris. Teasing him gently with a "Damn those bankers! Whatever shall we do? Well, if we must, Paris it is!"

He laughed heartily, as a big grin spread across his baby face, and I had to mention that this would be my first time visiting, so he knew to take it very, very seriously.

Opening my email, I found a message from his assistant with a business class ticket and expenses to ensure I arrived happy and in luxury. The thoughtfulness immediately set me at ease knowing full well I would be in good hands and well taken care of. Packing my sultriest dresses, I constructed a relaxed and sexy Parisian style for the first week of our trip and threw in oversized sweaters for fall in cape town. The anticipation of a romantic two weeks in exotic cities and luxury hotels wrapped in the arms of a delicious man had me excited and nervous.

The flight was relaxing, having spent most of it fast asleep in 'lay flat mode', one of the luxuries of a wealthy life. I was met at the airport by a driver holding a placard with my name on it. Malik called, apologetic at being unable to pick me up, but he had assured me his business was completed and he was now free to give me his full attention.

Pulling up to the boutique hotel, he stood out front, wrapping up a phone call. Opening my door, I beamed a huge smile at him, as he took my hand to help me out. I had forgotten how big he was, towering over me at 6'3, and with the stature of an

African black rhino. Thoughts of mounting him swam through my mind and being unable to hide my desire he responded with, "My god Bex! That look. Oh, how I missed you."

As I giggled with yearning, he pulled me in for a kiss, the world around us disappearing. The heat between us erupted, as I felt my body encircled in a fog of spice. A horn blared from behind, pulling us back to reality, and he took my hand to lead us out of the street.

The boutique hotel situated a few blocks from the Arc de Triomphe was understated, and having already checked us in, he gave me a key to my room.

"I thought you might prefer your own space.

Why don't you get cleaned up and then we can head out for dinner? I know you mentioned you like caviar. I have a treat for you" he added with a sly smile.

"Sounds perfect!" I beamed, in need of a shower after my fifteen-hour flight, and giddy at the promise of a caviar-filled night.

After my luggage arrived, I prepared myself for the evening, showering, unpacking, and picking the perfect attire for a luxury dinner. Slipping into a pink silk slip dress, and Gianvito Rossi black kitten heels, I checked my lipstick before heading down to meet him in the lobby. He had changed into a crisply pressed dark blue dress shirt, his monogram initials sewn elegantly into the cuff. Custom clothing was another luxury of the wealthy, and I pointed to his initials teasing him with "Fancy!"

"You know, I get all my shirts custom-made, so the little touches are very nice indeed." He responded.

"I can tell," I said, reaching over to wrap my arm through his and stroking the stiff material. "It fits you perfectly!"

He smiled down at me, the spice beginning to build between us once again. This spice was a collision of our energies, that had blossomed into a haze of heat, desire, passion, and sex. We were surrounded by it, so much so that he felt compelled to point it out.

"You look stunning, Bex. I don't know what to call it, but we have this energy when we get together. I felt it when we were in Johannesburg last summer and I have been obsessing over it. It draws me to you, and it feels so sweet and incredible to be in it."

"I feel the same. I know exactly what you are talking about. I have nicknamed it "The Spice". I replied.

"Yes! The spice. I like that. That is exactly how it feels. We are surrounded and suspended in it. This is new to me" He responded.

"I have not felt this before either. And it feels incredible. I know it's our energy meeting, but my god, the spice! It is the most delicious feeling." I laughed. Leaning in, he kissed my juicy lips, the torrent of spice whirling around us.

The driver was waiting out front, and as we stepped into the Mercedes, my excitement was etched across my face at the thought of the night to come.

"I hope you like *Caviar Kaspia.* It is a favorite spot of mine," he said.

My joy was overwhelming, as my face attempted to widen my already-plastered smile, forcing me to shake my arms in childish delight.

"As you can see, I have no control over myself right now!" I laughed, poking fun at my reaction.

"I like it. I think it's real. It's honest. It makes you even more beautiful, and it brings me joy to watch!" He answered, our eyes locked in a moment of vulnerability. I took his hand in mine, stroking the giant palm, intertwining my fingers in his.

"Thank you. I'm happy I can be myself." I smiled tenderly.

I had no desire to mask and refused to be with anyone that pushed me to be anything but myself.

Arriving at our destination, the blue and cream exterior of the restaurant was lit with fairy lights, the twinkle of a thousand little bulbs inviting us in. The host stepped forward extending his hand with a "Bienvenu Monsieur Serer," before whisking us up the stairs to the second-floor dining room. The opulent decor had an old-world shabbiness, the powder blue linens clashing slightly with the brown and cream chairs. We were seated in a semi-private section amongst a row of other couples, bodies leaning in and attentive to their partners. Glancing down towards the window, he said "I apologize. We were supposed to have that table at the end, but they said it is already reserved. I wonder who it is for? I always get that table."

Seeing his minor irritability, I replied "It's quite alright. I am just happy to be here. It must be someone very important. And at least now, you will know where you stand in the *Caviar Kaspia* pecking order." I laughed, making light of the situation.

He chuckled responding "Bex! I like the way you look at things. You have me laughing every time."

"Humor is good for the soul, and laughter is even better. Finding the right perspective in life will save you a lot of pain and heartbreak. I think at this point it is a coping mechanism, but I have to say, it works. I am still sane!" I replied, laughing more. Our eyes stared, bodies enjoying that feeling of peace and connection.

Turning our attention to the menu, he said "If it is alright with you, I would like to order for us."

"I would be delighted if you did. Thank you." I answered, happy to take a break from having to think, plan, and organize. It was *Caviar Kaspia* after all, so no matter what was ordered, it was going to be delicious. Addressing the waiter in French, his accent had no hint of his West African roots, and I admired how comfortable he was in the environment. I had to always remind myself I belonged, having always felt like an outsider or a fraud in spaces that did not have people who looked like me, which was most places.

With an *"Excellente!"* The waiter gave his approval of the order, taking away our menus.

Malik leaned in, reaching across the table and searching for my hand. I met him in the middle, grasping his and smiling.

"I think you are going to enjoy this. For the first course, we will have smoked salmon, followed by Osetra caviar. I refrained from ordering the baked potato. I think it's a mediocre accompaniment and just takes away from the feast of caviar!" he explained.

"I could not have said it better myself. Potatoes are just useless filler. Bring on the caviar! I'm so excited. Thank you!" I exclaimed, my face mock drooling from the description.

The waiter arrived with a bottle of *Dom Perignon* Brut champagne, and I was pleased he picked the perfect accompaniment to caviar.

Lifting our glasses to toast, he said "Cheers to us! To finding each other again."

"Cheers!" I replied. "It has been a gift. Thank you again!" Taking a sip, the bubbles tickled my nose, as the crisp dry liquid poured over my tongue. The feeling was heaven as my body relaxed, leaning back into the seat. "That's delicious!" I purred, licking the drops from my lips. He was chuckling, leading me

71

to ask, 'What are you laughing about now?'

"You! I like the way you enjoy life. You express it on your face, in your body. It's like it is coming out of your soul. I enjoy watching you" he answered.

I blushed momentarily and then threw him a wink and a laugh. "Well good. This is my first time in Paris, and I want to enjoy every moment of it, without restriction. I will not let anything ruin this. I am sitting across from a handsome man and about to enjoy a feast of caviar. Life is beautiful, and I am beyond blessed."

He smiled in response, tenderly squeezing and stroking my fingers, that feeling of spice floating around us. Breaking his gaze, I peered over towards the window, noticing the reserved table had finally been seated. Nodding my head in their direction I said, "It looks like your mystery guest is here. I wonder who it is."

Peering over, his eyes widened, and the look of surprise made me stare, ever more curious.

"It is a French minister. You would not know him. And that is certainly not his wife" he said.

My face lit up with intrigue, and the knowledge that a secret or maybe not-so-secret tryst was unfolding before us.

"Ooh, spicy!" I cooed, a sentiment dripping in mischief. "Well, I guess you have your answer then. Government trumps business, huh? He does have the power to shut this place down, so don't feel too bad about it" I teased.

"That is true, Bex. Good point. That is a power I do not care for. He can have it." he laughed congenially.

The waiter arrived with thin slices of smoked salmon laid delicately across a logo-embossed plate. Large crepe blini's stacked next to a silver bowl of crème fraiche with lemons, had my eyes as wide as saucers. I was a kid in a candy store, my whole body wiggling with anticipation of the first bite. The creamy flavors of the crème fraiche mixed with the tart lemon and smokey rich texture of the salmon took me back to childhood, the memory of eating Sunday morning bagels and lox with my Jewish grandparents. You know a dish is good when you are swimming in nostalgia.

Next up, came the caviar, which was presented in an oversized gold and black Matryoshka doll, her eyes closed as if in respite. Opening the vessel, the crystal bowl was filled with little black caviar pearls nestled on a bed of crushed ice, a portion meant for true indulgence.

Looking at Malik I announced "I can die now. This experience has made my life complete." He laughed and handed me a tiny spoon made of mother of pearl. I had learned from my many lessons in the restaurant business that Caviar must always be eaten with pearl spoons as metal ones impart an undesirable flavor. Scooping a giant blob of the fish roe, I placed it in my mouth, my eyes rolling into the back of my head. I delighted in the pop of texture as each piece burst in my mouth, dousing it in that delicious creamy brininess you can only ever experience with Osetra. The wave of pleasure that ran through my body culminated in a satisfied sigh. "Absolute heaven" I commented, drifting in the bliss of a good meal and spicy company.

Forgoing the blini, I continued spooning dollops of caviar straight into my mouth, purring with each bite.

"My god Bex. To watch you eat is even a pleasure" he said.

Feeling extra saucy, I cocked my head, and with a statement dripping in innuendo I replied,

"I know what I would like to watch you eat."

He chuckled, blushing through his ebony cheeks, and answered "Check?"

I nodded yes, our eyes glowing with the desire to touch.

As we exited the restaurant I turned to Malik, thanking him for an exceptional meal.

Pulling me into his embrace, his lips were soft, tender, and plump. His wet tongue dove deep into my mouth, searching to pull me into him. My body lit up as my pussy twinged at the ever-building spice. Pulling himself away, he had a wild look of desire that threatened to push the bounds of acceptable public displays of affection.

"The things I want to do to you right now Bex" he muttered through gritted teeth.

Leading us over to the car, Malik held the door, watching me hungrily as I situated myself in the back seat. I threw him a sly sexy glance, my message loud and clear, that I too was going to devour him. The ride back to the hotel was strained, both of us holding back, knowing that once we were unleashed, nothing could stop us.

He held my hand, squeezing and stroking, the sexual tension between us building into a ball of sparks in our fingers.

"I want to take you right now, but the windows have eyes," he spoke.

"Meaning?" I asked teasingly. "Who is watching?"

He glanced over at the driver and replied "Everyone. You must always be careful in Paris. People talk!"

"Let them talk!" I laughed brazenly. "No. I'm joking. The last thing I want is to put on a show for strangers."

Pulling up to the hotel, we hurriedly exited the car, ran through the lobby, and laughed as we simultaneously pushed the elevator button.

Stepping in, he looked around to make sure there were no

cameras and then pulled me into his orbit. Locking his lips with mine, our tongues weaved in and out, furiously attempting to taste, touch, and consume each other. Wrapping my arms around his torso, I rubbed circles into his back and felt him relax against me. We were lost in each other when the slow elevator finally dinged, announcing our floor. Spilling into his hotel room, I felt his big hands rub down my slip dress, reaching around to grab my ass. The sensation sent a spark through me, making my pussy wet. My desire was overflowing, and I wanted his dick in my mouth.

Letting the silk dress slide off my body, he reached down and pulled my panties off. I kissed his collarbone, chest, belly, and thigh before kneeling fully in front of his hard cock. Staring up into his eyes, I darted my tongue out to lick the very tip of his penis. His breath caught in his throat as he sucked in heavily, a deep groan pouring from his chest. Wrapping my lips around the tip, I played with the soft skin, languishing in his heavy groans. Reaching over to my purse, I pulled out a mini vibrator and placed it against my clitoris. Staring up at him I said, "I want you to fuck my mouth".

"Oh god, Bex. You turn me on so much" he replied wide-eyed.

Wrapping my mouth around his dick once again, I sucked it in and hit the button on my vibrator. The sensation kicked me into another stratosphere, as my body responded to the intense pleasure. He gently moved his hips back and forth, breathing through his teeth with each stroke. I wanted more, so I grabbed his hand and placed it on the back of my head, pushing him deeper into my mouth. With lips full of cock, I mumbled: "fuck my mouth!" The directive sent his hips bucking as he held my head and fucked faster. I was in heaven as the soft skin danced in and out of my mouth and his cock filled it with each thrust.

My pussy was sopping wet, the liquid dripping between my legs as the pleasure built, sending shock waves. The vibrator buzzed rapidly as I reveled in the orgasm washing over me. Malik grasped my head harder, holding his dick in the back of my throat, the vibrations of my moans sending him into a frantic pace. The hot liquid shot out, and I swallowed it quickly, my body floundering limply against his legs. Taking my arms, he lifted me easily, and we sprawled across the bed, bathing in the waves of our pleasure.

"Bex, I feel like a wild man with you. I want more," he spoke.

"The night is young. That was just round one." I said, curling up into his side and resting my head against his chest. Cuddling, I stroked him, pinching his nipples in between my fingers. His body responded, twitching and a little gasp slipped from his lips. Leaning down, I put his nipple in my mouth and sucked on the hard bud. Another loud gasp punctured the air, and he writhed under the sensation. Laying my body on top of his, I straddled his hips and laid his penis in between the soft lips of my pussy. The wetness made him slip back and forth as I rocked my hips against him. His eyes rolled back, and I could see he was lost once again, drifting in pleasure. Rubbing my pert breasts against his chest, I captured his lips in mine, biting them. The repeated moan of pleasure spurred me to continue rubbing and grinding. Lifting my hips, I grabbed his cock and placed the tip in my pussy, dipping it in and out repeatedly. His voice grew louder, as my hips teased, grinding against him. Grabbing the headboard behind him, I plunged downward engulfing the shaft, a long-drawn-out sob rumbling from his lips. Squeezing my pussy to wrap fully around his cock, I moved quickly, pounding, and then grinding, enjoying the tantalizing feel of his hard penis as it hit just the right spot.

The grinding rubbed my clitoris against his belly, a delicious sensation in combination with each thrust. Our bodies were on fire, the feel and scent of spice had us locked in our world of pure bliss. He reached up, tweaking my nipple, and a rush of pain shot through me, which dissipated into pleasure. It was just the right amount to pull me out of the haze of spice and into full-blown orgasm. My body erupted as I experienced 'the trifecta'; aptly nicknamed because it is achieved through the stimulation of three erogenous zones, the result sending one out of this world. The sensation of nipple, clitoris, and pussy simultaneously thrumming. With the squeeze of a nipple, I was shot out of the orgasmic cannon, my body flailing with intense pleasure and the sensation of weightlessness. Collapsing next to him, I lay panting, sweat glistening across my skin. Reaching over for the glass of water on the bedside table, I lifted it to take a sip. The glass instantly slipped through my fingers, smashing to the floor below; my body weak and spent from such an intense orgasm. "Shit" was all I could muster, before adding "You see what you do to me?"

He laughed at the accusation replying "Don't move. I got you" Cleaning up the shards of glass he laid a fresh towel on the carpet to ensure I did not get cut.

"I am so sorry. I don't know how that happened. It just felt like my arms didn't work." I added apologetically.

"Bex, please do not apologize. These things happen. And as you said, look what I do to you!" He laughed. "Such power in my hands. How shall I wield it?" he quipped, positioning himself at the end of the bed.

Grabbing my legs, he slid my body down the bed, staring intently at my thighs. Spreading them, he maneuvered his head in between, and dipped his nose, rubbing his lips across the soft skin. His large lips placed kisses that felt like plush pillows pressing against my pussy. A hard tongue darted out, opening the folds, and stroking my clitoris. An electric current surged from the little nub, a spasm ripping through my body. Reaching for his head, I wrapped my thighs tighter and ground my pussy deeper. His eyes widened and reaching up to grab my ass with one hand, he flipped us over so that I was sitting on his face. Surprised by the quick maneuver, I felt a rush of endorphins heighten my pleasure, driving me to ride him. His ecstatic gasps told me he was enjoying himself. Reaching behind me, I rubbed down his belly to grab his hard cock, stroking it and continued to fuck his mouth, my pussy swollen with desire. Rubbing hot wet circles into his face, his body began to contort, clenching as he squirmed under the weight of my ass. His hips jutted up to meet each stroke of my hand, the pressure of my fingers, squeezing until he bellowed from between my thighs. With each sound, I pumped my hips faster, his tongue stuffed in my pussy, furiously lapping. The weightlessness of orgasm sent my mind floating into space as his cock spurt hot cum into the air, and I felt it sprinkle across my hand, dripping down onto his stomach. Toppling onto the bed, we lay panting in the heat of our spice. Reaching over to the nightstand, he handed me a wet towel. "Thank you!" I said, cleaning my fingers before handing it back.

"Wow, Bex! That was truly incredible. I know it must be a cliche, but I need a cigarette!" He laughed.

Handing me a white luxury robe, he picked up his cigarettes and led the way into the en suite living room. We were situated on the top floor of the hotel, the windows opening to gray shingled roof slats and a view of the Eiffel Tower. Lit with white lights that glowed against the night sky, he turned to me, his eyes becoming serious and his deep baritone voice saying "I had a marvelous time. I find you beautiful, body and soul, which in this barbaric world of ours is a blessing wrapped in prowess. I know our time together has been brief, but I view it as an opportunity for us to meet again in nigh times as opposed to allowing fate to intervene. This is a rain check and would be redeemable in law and fact. Thereby empowering schedules and the vagaries of life."

My face lit up in laughter as I processed his words. "What a romantic way to say 'I want to see you again'" I replied. "Well, I want to see you again too." Our eyes locked in a joyful connection, the beam of desire drawing us into a slow, long heated kiss, full of spice and dreams of adventures to come.

Afterword

Glossary of Terms

1. **Diddly Tale:** A story that awakens sexual desire and leads to masturbation. To Diddle oneself is to touch one's erogenous zones to orgasm.
2. **Meze**: Small plates and appetizers that are shared before the main meal in the Middle East.
3. **Iskender**: A Turkish dish that consists of sliced doner kebab meat topped with hot tomato sauce over pita bread, and generously slathered with sheep's milk butter.
4. **Pakol/Pakul**: A soft, flat, rolled up, round-topped men's cap usually worn in Afghanistan and Pakistan.
5. **Kangol Bucket Hat:** A bucket style hat made by the Kangol British Company, founded in 1938. This style emerged as a major fashion trend in the 1980's and 90's after it was popularized in the movie *New Jack City (1991).*
6. **AK47**: Officially known as the Avtomat Kalashnikova, the AK47 is a gas operated assault rifle developed in the Soviet Union by the Kalashnikov family.
7. **Omakase**: A Japanese phrase used when ordering food in restaurants that means "I'll leave it up to you". The word translation means "to entrust", giving the chef permission to select and serve seasonal specialties.

8. **Usuzukuri:** Fish that is sliced thinly. A traditional style in Japanese cuisine.
9. **Tamagoyaki:** A type of Japanese omelet made by rolling together several layers of egg and is often prepared in a special rectangular omelet pan called a *Makiyakinabe.*
10. **Tostada:** A flat toasted or deep fried tortilla used as a base in Mexican dishes. Traditionally topped with fish, shrimp or other type of protein.
11. **Chirashi/Chirashizushi:** Translates to "scattered sushi" and is a style of sushi that entails pieces of sashimi over a bowl of sushi rice.
12. **Kanpai:** A traditional Japanese drinking toast meaning "cheers" or "drink up".
13. **Osetra Caviar:** One of the most prized and expensive types of fish roe obtained from the Osetra sturgeon, which weighs 50-400 pounds and can live up to 50 years.

Bibliography

1. Deutch, Howard. *Pretty in Pink.* Performance by Molly Ringwald. Written by John Hughes. Paramount Pictures 1986.
2. "Diddle" *Urban Dictionary 2023.* Urbandictionary.com.
3. Forsey, Keith. Moroder, Giorgio. *What a Feeling.* Performed by Irene Cara. What a Feelin'/Flashdance: Original Soundtrack from the motion picture. Casablanca,

Network, 1983.

4. Gaye, Marvin. *Let's get it on.* Performed by Marvin Gaye. Let's get it on (Studio Album). Tamla, 1973.

5. Hughes, John. *Sixteen Candle.* Performance by Molly Ringwald. Universal Pictures, Channel Productions, 1984.

6. Hughes, John. *Breakfast Club.* Performance by Molly Ringwald. Universal Pictures, 1985.

7. Kipner, Steve. Shaddick, Terry. *Let's get physical.* Performance by Olivia Newton John. Physical. EMI/MCA, 1981.

8. Nin, Anais. *Delta of Venus: Erotica.* Harcourt Brace Jovanovich, 1977.

9. Rios, Christopher. Foster, Jerome. *Still Not a Player.* Performed by Big Pun and Joe. Loud RCA, 1998.

About the Author

Bex Kesia is a writer of erotic adventure stories. Follow @bexkesia on Instagram and @diddlytales on Tik Tok for updates on the second book in the Diddly Tales series.